BY EVELYN WAUGH

Novels
DECLINE AND FALL
VILE BODIES
BLACK MISCHIEF
A HANDFUL OF DUST
SCOOP
PUT OUT MORE FLAGS
WORK SUSPENDED
BRIDESHEAD REVISITED
SCOTT-KING'S MODERN EUROPE
THE LOVED ONE
HELENA
MEN AT ARMS
LOVE AMONG THE RUINS
OFFICERS AND GENTLEMEN
UNCONDITIONAL SURRENDER
THE ORDEAL OF GILBERT PINFOLD

Biography
ROSSETTI
EDMUND CAMPION
MSGR. RONALD KNOX

Autobiography
A LITTLE LEARNING

Travel
LABELS
REMOTE PEOPLE
NINETY-TWO DAYS
WAUGH IN ABYSSINIA
ROBBERY UNDER LAW
WHEN THE GOING WAS GOOD
A TOURIST IN AFRICA

Short Stories
MR. LOVEDAY'S LITTLE OUTING, AND OTHER SAD STORIES
BASIL SEAL RIDES AGAIN

VILE BODIES

VILE BODIES

by

EVELYN WAUGH

LITTLE, BROWN AND COMPANY · BOSTON

LIBRARY OF CONGRESS CATALOG CARD NO. 77–88240

REPUBLISHED OCTOBER 1977

PRINTED IN THE UNITED STATES OF AMERICA

"Well in our *country*," said Alice, still panting a little, "you'd generally get to somewhere else—if you ran very fast for a long time, as we've been doing."

"A slow sort of country!" said the Queen. "Now, here, you see, it takes all the running you can do, to keep in the same place. If you want to get somewhere else, you must run at least twice as fast as that!"

"If I wasn't real," Alice said—half laughing through her tears, it all seemed so ridiculous—"I shouldn't be able to cry."

"I hope you don't suppose those are real tears?" Tweedledum interrupted in a tone of great contempt.

—*Alice Through the Looking Glass.*

AUTHOR'S NOTE

TWO episodes from *Vile Bodies* have appeared, in a slightly different form, as short
stories in *The New Decameron* and *Harp-
er's Bazaar,* whose editors own the respective serial
rights.

The action of the book is laid in the near future,
when existing social tendencies have become more
marked; I have postulated no mechanical or scien-
tific advance, but in the interest of compactness and
with no pretensions to prophecy, I have assumed a
certain speeding up of legal procedure and daily
journalism. In the latter case I have supposed a
somewhat later hour for going to press and a greater
expedition in distribution than is now generally the
case.

All the characters and places mentioned, newspapers, hotels, night clubs, restaurants, motor cars,

etc., are wholly imaginary and, of course, titles such as Prime Minister, Archbishop of Canterbury, Home Secretary, etc., are used without any reference to present, past and future holders of the offices.

Vile Bodies is in no sense a sequel to *Decline and Fall*, though many of the same characters appear in both. I think, however, that some of the minor motives will be clearer to those who have read my first book than to those who have not.

It has been suggested to me that the chronology may be a little obscure. The book begins on November 10th, and the events of the first six sections occupied three days. The airship party and Lady Anchorage's reception were on the same night—December 2nd. The motor races were on December 5th. Adam's visit to the nursing home was on December 15th. Christmas is observed by the Western Church on December 25th.

E. W.

VILE BODIES

T was clearly going to be a bad crossing.

With Asiatic resignation Father Rothschild S.J. put down his suitcase in the corner of the bar and went on deck. (It was a small suitcase of imitation crocodile hide. The initials stamped on it in Gothic characters were not Father Rothschild's, for he had borrowed it that morning from the *valet-de-chambre* of his hotel. It contained some rudimentary underclothes, six important new books in six languages, a false beard and a school atlas and gazetteer heavily annotated.) Standing on the deck Father Rothschild leant his elbow on the rail, rested his chin in his hands and surveyed the procession of passengers coming up the gangway, each face eloquent of polite misgiving.

Very few of them were unknown to the Jesuit, for it was his happy knack to remember everything that could possibly be learned about everyone who could possibly be of any importance. His tongue protruded very slightly and, had they not all been so concerned with luggage and the weather, someone might have observed in him a peculiar resemblance to those plaster reproductions of the gargoyles of Notre Dame which may be seen in the shop windows of artists' colourmen tinted the colour of "Old Ivory," peering intently from among stencil outfits and plasticene and tubes of water-colour paint. High above his head swung Mrs. Melrose Ape's travel-worn Packard car, bearing the dust of three continents, against the darkening sky, and up the companion-way at the head of her angels strode Mrs. Melrose Ape, the woman evangelist.

"Faith."

"Here, Mrs. Ape."

"Charity."

"Here, Mrs. Ape."

"Fortitude."

"Here, Mrs. Ape."

"Chastity. . . . Where is Chastity?"

"Chastity didn't feel well, Mrs. Ape. She went below."

"That girl's more trouble than she's worth. When-

2

ever there's any packing to be done, Chastity doesn't feel well. Are all the rest here—Humility, Prudence, Divine Discontent, Mercy, Justice and Creative Endeavour?"

"Creative Endeavour lost her wings, Mrs. Ape. She got talking to a gentleman in the train. . . . Oh, there she is."

"Got 'em?" asked Mrs. Ape.

Too breathless to speak, Creative Endeavour nodded. (Each of the angels carried her wings in a little black box like a violin case.)

"Right," said Mrs. Ape, "and just you hold on to 'em tight and not so much talking to gentlemen in trains. You're angels, not a panto, see?"

The angels crowded together disconsolately. It was awful when Mrs. Ape was like this. My, how they would pinch Chastity and Creative Endeavour when they got them alone in their nightshirts. It was bad enough their going to be so sick without that they had Mrs. Ape pitching into them too.

Seeing their discomfort, Mrs. Ape softened and smiled. She was nothing if not "magnetic."

"Well, girls," she said, "I must be getting along. They say it's going to be rough, but don't you believe it. If you have peace in your hearts your stomach will

3

look after itself, and remember if you *do* feel queer—
sing. There's nothing like it."

"Good-bye, Mrs. Ape, and thank you," said the
angels; they bobbed prettily, turned about and
trooped aft to the second-class part of the ship. Mrs.
Ape watched them benignly, then, squaring her shoulders and looking (except that she had really no beard
to speak of) every inch a sailor, strode resolutely
forrard to the first-class bar.

Other prominent people were embarking, all very
unhappy about the weather; to avert the terrors of
sea-sickness they had indulged in every kind of civ-
ilized witchcraft, but they were lacking in faith.

Miss Runcible was there, and Miles Malpractice,
and all the Younger Set. They had spent a jolly morning strapping each other's tummies with sticking
plaster (how Miss Runcible had wriggled).

The Right Honourable Walter Outrage, M.P., last
week's Prime Minister, was there. Before breakfast
that morning (which had suffered in consequence)
Mr. Outrage had taken twice the maximum dose of
a patent preparation of chloral, and losing heart later
had finished the bottle in the train. He moved in an
uneasy trance, closely escorted by the most public-
4

looking detective sergeants. These men had been with Mr. Outrage in Paris, and what they did not know about his goings on was not worth knowing, at least from a novelist's point of view. (When they spoke about him to each other they called him "the Right *H*onourable Rape," but that was more by way of being a pun about his name than a criticism of the conduct of his love affairs, in which, if the truth were known, he displayed a notable diffidence and the liability to panic.)

Lady Throbbing and Mrs. Blackwater, those twin sisters whose portrait by Millais auctioned recently at Christie's made a record in rock-bottom prices, were sitting on one of the teak benches eating apples and drinking what Lady Throbbing, with late Victorian *chic*, called "a bottle of pop," and Mrs. Blackwater, more exotically, called *"champagne,"* pronouncing it as though it were French.

"Surely, Kitty, that is Mr. Outrage, last week's Prime Minister."

"Nonsense, Fanny, where?"

"Just in front of the two men with bowler hats, next to the clergyman."

"It is certainly like his photographs. How strange he looks."

"Just like poor Throbbing . . . all that last year."

". . . And none of us even suspected . . . until they found the bottles under the board in his dressing-room . . . and we all used to think it was drink . . ."

"I don't think one finds *quite* the same class as Prime Minister nowadays, do you think?"

"They say that only *one* person has any influence with Mr. Outrage . . ."

"At the Japanese Embassy . . ."

"Of course, dear, not so loud. But tell me, Fanny, seriously, do you think really and truly Mr. Outrage has IT?"

"He has a very nice figure for a man of his age."

"Yes, but *his age*, and the bull-like type is so often disappointing. Another glass? You will be grateful for it when the ship begins to move."

"I quite thought we *were* moving."

"How absurd you are, Fanny, and yet I can't help laughing."

So arm in arm and shaken by little giggles the two tipsy old ladies went down to their cabin.

Of the other passengers, some had filled their ears with cotton wool, others wore smoked glasses, while several ate dry captain's biscuits from paper bags, as

6

Red Indians are said to eat snake's flesh to make them cunning. Mrs. Hoop repeated feverishly over and over again a formula she had learned from a yogi in New York City. A few "good sailors," whose luggage bore the labels of many voyages, strode aggressively about smoking small, foul pipes and trying to get up a four of bridge.

Two minutes before the advertised time of departure, while the first admonitory whistling and shouting was going on, a young man came on board carrying his bag. There was nothing particularly remarkable about his appearance. He looked exactly as young men like him do look; he was carrying his own bag, which was disagreeably heavy, because he had no money left in francs and very little left in anything else. He had been two months in Paris writing a book and was coming home because, in the course of his correspondence, he had got engaged to be married. His name was Adam Fenwick-Symes.

Father Rothschild smiled at him in a kindly manner.

"I doubt whether you remember me," he said. "We met at Oxford five years ago at luncheon with the Dean of Balliol. I shall be interested to read your book when it appears—an autobiography, I understand. And may I be one of the first to congratulate you on your engagement? I am afraid you will find your father-in-law a little eccentric—and forgetful. He had a nasty attack of bronchitis this winter. It is a draughty house—far too big for these days. Well, I must go below now. It is going to be rough and I am a bad sailor. We meet at Lady Metroland's on the twelfth, if not, as I hope, before."

Before Adam had time to reply the Jesuit disappeared. Suddenly the head popped back.

"There is an extremely dangerous and disagreeable woman on board—a Mrs. Ape."

Then he was gone again, and almost at once the boat began to slip away from the quay towards the mouth of the harbour.

Sometimes the ship pitched and sometimes she rolled and sometimes she stood quite still and shivered all over, poised above an abyss of dark water; then she would go swooping down like a scenic railway train into a windless hollow and up again with a rush into the gale; sometimes she would burrow her path, with convulsive nosings and scramblings like a terrier in a rabbit hole; and sometimes she would

8

drop dead like a lift. It was this last movement that caused the most havoc among the passengers.

"Oh," said the Bright Young People, "Oh, oh, oh."

"It's just exactly like being inside a cocktail shaker," said Miles Malpractice. "Darling, your face —eau de Nil."

"Too, too sick-making," said Miss Runcible, with one of her rare flashes of accuracy.

Kitty Blackwater and Fanny Throbbing lay one above the other in their bunks rigid from wig to toe.

"I wonder, do you think the *champagne* . . . ?"

"Kitty."

"Yes, Fanny, dear."

"Kitty, I think, in fact, I am sure I have some sal volatile. . . . Kitty, I thought that perhaps as you are nearer . . . it would really hardly be safe for me to try and descend . . . I might break a leg."

"Not after *champagne*, Fanny, do you think?"

"But I need it. Of course, dear, *if it's too much trouble?*"

"Nothing is too much trouble, darling, you know that. But now I come to think of it, I remember, quite clearly, for a fact, that you did *not* pack the sal volatile."

"Oh, Kitty, oh, Kitty, please . . . you would be sorry for this if I died . . . oh."

"But I saw the sal volatile on your dressing-table after your luggage had gone down, dear. I remember thinking, I must take that down to Fanny, and then, dear, I got confused over the tips, so you see . . ."

"I . . . put . . . it . . . in . . . myself. . . . ,Next to my brushes . . . you . . . beast."

"Oh, Fanny . . ."

"Oh . . . Oh . . . Oh."

To Father Rothschild no passage was worse than any other. He thought of the sufferings of the saints, the mutability of human nature, the Four Last Things, and between whiles repeated snatches of the penitential psalms.

The Leader of His Majesty's Opposition lay sunk in a rather glorious coma, made splendid by dreams of Oriental imagery—of painted paper houses; of golden dragons and gardens of almond blossom; of golden limbs and almond eyes, humble and caressing; of very small golden feet among almond blossoms; of little painted cups full of golden tea; of a golden voice singing behind a painted paper screen; of humble, caressing little golden hands and eyes shaped like almonds and the colour of night.

Outside his door two very limp detective sergeants had deserted their posts.

"The bloke as could make trouble on a ship like this 'ere deserves to get away with it," they said.

The ship creaked in every plate, doors slammed, trunks fell about, the wind howled; the screw, now out of the water, now in, raced and churned, shaking down hat-boxes like ripe apples; but above all the roar and clatter there rose from the second-class ladies' saloon the despairing voices of Mrs. Ape's angels, in frequently broken unison, singing, singing, wildly, desperately, as though their hearts would break in the effort and their minds lose their reason, Mrs. Ape's famous hymn, *There ain't no flies on the Lamb of God.*

The Captain and the Chief Officer sat on the bridge engrossed in a crossword puzzle.

"Looks like we may get some heavy weather if the wind gets up," he said. "Shouldn't wonder if there wasn't a bit of a sea running tonight."

"Well, we can't always have it quiet like this," said the Chief Officer. "Word of eighteen letters meaning

11

carnivorous mammal. Search me if I know how they do think of these things."

Adam Fenwick-Symes sat among the good sailors in the smoking-room drinking his third Irish whisky and wondering how soon he would feel definitely ill. Already there was a vague depression gathering at the top of his head. There were thirty-five minutes more, probably longer with the head wind keeping them back.

Opposite him sat a much-travelled and chatty journalist telling him smutty stories. From time to time Adam interposed some more or less appropriate comment, "No, I say that's a good one," or, "I must remember that," or just, "Ha, Ha, Ha," but his mind was not really in a receptive condition.

Up went the ship, up, up, up, paused and then plunged down with a sidelong slither. Adam caught at his glass and saved it. Then shut his eyes.

"Now I'll tell you a drawing-room one," said the journalist.

Behind them a game of cards was in progress among the commercial gents. At first they had rather a jolly time about it, saying, "What ho, she bumps," or "Steady, the Bluffs," when the cards and glasses and ash-tray were thrown on to the floor, but in the last ten minutes they were growing notably quieter. It was rather a nasty kind of hush.

". . . And forty aces and two-fifty for the rubber. Shall we cut again or stay as we are?"

"How about knocking off for a bit? Makes me tired —table moving about all the time."

"Why, Arthur, you ain't feeling ill, surely?"

" 'Course I ain't feeling ill, only tired."

"Well, of course, if Arthur's feeling ill . . ."

"Who'd have thought of old Arthur feeling ill?"

"I ain't feeling ill, I tell you. Just tired. But if you boys want to go on I'm not the one to spoil a game."

"Good old Arthur. 'Course he ain't feeling ill. Look out for the cards, Bill, up she goes again."

"What about one all round? Same again?"

"Same again."

"Good luck, Arthur." "Good luck." "Here's fun." "Down she goes."

"Whose deal? You dealt last, didn't you, Mr. Henderson?' '

"Yes, Arthur's deal."

"Your deal, Arthur. Cheer up, old scout."

"Don't you go doing that. It isn't right to hit a chap on the back like that."

13

"Look out with the cards, Arthur."

"Well, what d'you expect, being hit on the back like that. Makes me tired."

"Here, I got fifteen cards."

"I wonder if you've heard this one," said the journalist. "There was a man lived at Aberdeen, and he was terribly keen on fishing, so when he married, he married a woman with worms. That's rich, eh? You see he was keen on fishing, see, and she had worms, see, he lived in Aberdeen. That's a good one, that is."

"D'you know, I think I shall go on deck for a minute. A bit stuffy in here, don't you think?"

"You can't do that. The sea's coming right over it all the time. Not feeling queer, are you?"

"No, of course I'm not feeling queer. I only thought a little fresh air. . . . Christ, why won't the damn thing stop?"

"Steady, old boy. I wouldn't go trying to walk about, not if I were you. Much better stay just where you are. What you want's a spot of whisky."

"Not feeling ill, you know. Just stuffy."

"That's all right, old boy. Trust Auntie."

The bridge party was not being a success.

"Hullo, Mr. Henderson. What's that spade?"

"That's the ace, that is."

14

"I can see it's the ace. What I mean you didn't ought to have trumped that last trick not if you had a spade."

"What d'you mean, didn't ought to have trumped it? Trumps led."

"No, they did *not*. Arthur led a spade."

"He led a trump, didn't you, Arthur?"

"Arthur led a spade."

"He couldn't have led a spade because for why he put a heart on my king of spades when I thought he had the queen. He hasn't got no spades."

"What d'you mean, not got no spades? I got the queen."

"Arthur, old man, you *must* be feeling queer."

"No, I ain't, I tell you, just tired. You'd be tired if you'd been hit on the back same as I was . . . anyway I'm fed up with this game . . . there go the cards again."

This time no one troubled to pick them up. Presently Mr. Henderson said, "Funny thing, don't know why I feel all swimmy of a sudden. Must have ate something that wasn't quite right. You never can tell with foreign foods—all messed up like they do."

"Now you mention it, I don't feel too spry myself. Damn bad ventilation on these Channel boats."

15

"That's what it is. Ventilation. You said it."

"You know I'm funny. I never feel sea-sick, mind, but I often find going on boats doesn't agree with me."

"I'm like that, too."

"Ventilation . . . a disgrace."

"Lord, I shall be glad when we get to Dover. Home, sweet home, eh?"

Adam held on very tightly to the brass-bound edge of the table and felt a little better. He was *not* going to be sick, and that was that; not with that gargoyle of a man opposite anyway. They *must* be in sight of land soon.

It was at this time, when things were at their lowest, that Mrs. Ape reappeared in the smoking-room. She stood for a second or two in the entrance balanced between swinging door and swinging door-post; then as the ship momentarily righted herself, she strode to the bar, her feet well apart, her hands in the pockets of her tweed coat.

"Double rum," she said and smiled magnetically at the miserable little collection of men seated about the room. "Why, boys," she said, "but you're looking terrible put out over something. What's it all about? Is it your souls that's wrong or is it that the ship won't

16

keep still? Rough? 'Course it's rough. But let me ask you this. If you're put out this way over just an hour's sea-sickness" ("Not sea-sick, ventilation," said Mr. Henderson mechanically) "what are you going to be like when you make the mighty big journey that's waiting for us all? Are you right with God?" said Mrs. Ape. "Are you prepared for death?"

"Oh, am I not?" said Arthur. "I 'aven't thought of nothing else for the last half hour."

"Now, boys, I'll tell you what we're going to do. We're going to sing a song together, you and me." ("Oh, God," said Adam.) "You may not know it, but you are. You'll feel better for it body *and* soul. It's a song of Hope. You don't hear much about Hope these days, do you? Plenty about Faith, plenty about Charity. They've forgotten all about Hope. There's only one great evil in the world today. Despair. I know all about England, and I tell you straight, boys, I've got the goods for you. Hope's what you want and Hope's what I got. Here, steward, hand round these leaflets. There's the song on the back. Now all together . . . sing. Five bob for you, steward, if you can shout me down. Splendid, all together, boys."

In a rich, very audible voice Mrs. Ape led the singing. Her arms rose, fell and fluttered with the rhythm

17

of the song. The bar steward was hers already—inaccurate sometimes in his reading of the words, but with a sustained power in the low notes that defied competition. The journalist joined in next and Arthur set up a little hum. Soon they were all at it, singing like blazes, and it is undoubtedly true that they felt the better for it.

Father Rothschild heard it and turned his face to the wall.

Kitty Blackwater heard it.
"Fanny."
"Well."
"Fanny, dear, do you hear singing?"
"Yes, dear, thank you."
"Fanny, dear, I hope they aren't holding a *service*. I mean, dear, it sounds so like a hymn. Do you think, possibly, we are *in danger?* Fanny, are we going to be wrecked?"
"I should be neither surprised nor sorry."
"Darling, how can you? . . . We should have heard it, shouldn't we, if we had actually *hit* anything? . . . Fanny, dear, if you like I will have a look for your sal volatile."

18

"I hardly think that would be any help, dear, since you *saw* it on my dressing-table."

"I may have been mistaken."

"You *said* you *saw* it."

The captain heard it. "All the time I been at sea," he said, "I never could stand for missionaries."

"Word of six letters beginning with ZB," said the chief officer, "meaning 'used in astronomic calculations.'"

"Z can't be right," said the captain after a few minutes' thought.

The Bright Young People heard it. "So like one's first parties," said Miss Runcible, "being sick with other people singing."

Mrs. Hoop heard it. "Well," she thought, "I'm through with theosophy after this journey. Reckon I'll give the Catholics the once over."

Aft, in the second-class saloon, where the screw was doing its worst, the Angels heard it. It was some time since they had given up singing.

"Her again," said Divine Discontent.

Mr. Outrage alone lay happily undisturbed, his mind absorbed in lovely dream sequences of a world of little cooing voices, so caressing, so humble; and dark eyes, night-coloured, the shape of almonds over painted paper screens; little golden bodies, so flexible, so firm, so surprising in the positions they assumed.

They were still singing in the smoking-room when, in very little more than her usual time, the ship came into the harbour at Dover. Then Mrs. Ape, as was her invariable rule, took round the hat and collected nearly two pounds, not counting her own five shillings which she got back from the bar steward. "Salvation doesn't do them the same good if they think it's free," was her favourite axiom.

II

AVE you anything to declare?"

"Wings."

"Have you wore them?"

"Sure."

"That's all right, then."

"Divine Discontent gets all the smiles all the time," complained Fortitude to Prudence. "Golly, but it's good to be on dry land."

Unsteadily, but with renewed hope, the passengers had disembarked.

Father Rothschild fluttered a diplomatic *laissez-passer* and disappeared in the large car that had been sent to meet him. The others were jostling one another with their luggage, trying to attract the Customs officers and longing for a cup of tea.

"I got half a dozen of the best stowed away," confided the journalist. "They're generally pretty easy

21

after a bad crossing." And sure enough he was soon settled in the corner of a first-class carriage (for the paper was, of course, paying his expenses) with his luggage safely chalked in the van.

It was some time before Adam could get attended to.

"I've nothing but some very old clothes and some books," he said.

But here he showed himself deficient in tact, for the man's casual air disappeared in a flash.

"Books, eh?" he said. "And what sort of books, may I ask?"

"Look for yourself."

"Thank *you*, that's what I mean to do. *Books*, indeed."

Adam wearily unstrapped and unlocked his suitcase.

"Yes," said the Customs officer menacingly, as though his worst suspicions had been confirmed, "I should just about say you had got some books."

One by one he took the books out and piled them on the counter. A copy of Dante's *Purgatorio* excited his especial disgust.

"French, eh?" he said. "I guessed as much, and pretty dirty, too, I shouldn't wonder. Now just you wait while I look up these here *books*"—how he said it!—"in my list. Particularly against books the Home Secretary is. If we can't stamp out literature in the country, we can at least stop its being brought in from outside. That's what he said the other day in Parliament, and I says 'Hear, hear. . . .' Hullo, hullo, what's this, may I ask?"

Gingerly, as though it might at any moment explode, he produced and laid on the counter a large pile of typescript.

"That's a book, too," said Adam. "One I've just written. It is my memoirs."

"Ho, it is, is it? Well, I'll take that along, too, to the chief. You better come too."

"But I've got to catch the train."

"You come along. There's worse things than missing trains," he hinted darkly.

They went together into an inner office, the walls of which were lined with contraband pornography and strange instruments, whose purpose Adam could not guess. From the next room came the shrieks and yells of poor Miss Runcible, who had been mistaken for a well-known jewel smuggler, and was being stripped to the skin by two terrific wardresses.

"Now then, what's this about books?" said the chief.

With the help of a printed list, which began "Aristotle, Works of (Illustrated)," they went through Adam's books, laboriously, one at a time, spelling out the titles.

Miss Runcible came through the office, working hard with lipstick and compact.

"Adam, darling, I never saw you on the boat," she said. "My dear, I can't *tell* you the *things* that have been happening to me in there. The way they looked . . . too, too shaming. Positively surgical, my dear, and *such* wicked old women, just like *Dowagers*, my dear. As soon as I get to London I shall just ring up every Cabinet Minister and *all* the newspapers and give them all the most shy-making details."

The chief was at this time engrossed in Adam's memoirs, giving vent at intervals to a sinister chuckling sound that was partly triumphant and partly derisive, but in the main genuinely appreciative.

"Coo, Bert," he said. "Look at this; that's rich, ain't it?"

Presently he collected the sheets, tied them together and put them on one side.

"Well, see here," he said. "You can take these books on architecture and the dictionary, and I don't mind stretching a point for once and letting you have the

24

history books too. But this book on Economics comes under Subversive Propaganda. That you leaves behind. And this here *Purgatorio* doesn't look right to me, so that stays behind, pending inquiries. But as for this autobiography, that's just downright dirt, and we burns that straight away, see."

"But good heavens, there isn't a word in the book —you must be misinterpreting it."

"Not so much of it. I knows dirt when I sees it or I shouldn't be where I am today."

"But do you realize that my whole livelihood depends on this book?"

"And *my* livelihood depends on stopping works like this coming into the country. Now 'ook it quick if you don't want a police-court case."

"Adam, angel, don't fuss or we shall miss the train."

Miss Runcible took his arm and led him back to the station and told him all about a lovely party that was going to happen that night.

"*Queer*, who felt queer?"
"You did, Arthur."
"No I never . . . just tired."
"It certainly was stuffy in there just for a bit."

"Wonderful how that old girl cheered things up. Got a meeting next week in the Albert Hall."

"Shouldn't be surprised if I didn't go. What do you say, Mr. Henderson?"

"She got a troupe of angels, so she said. All dressed up in white with wings, lovely. Not a bad-looker herself, if it comes to that."

"What did you put in the plate, Arthur?"

"Half-crown."

"So did I. Funny thing I ain't never give half-crown like that before. She kind of draws it out of you, damned if she doesn't."

"You won't get away from the Albert Hall not without putting your hand in your pocket."

"No, but I'd like to see those angels dressed up, eh, Mr. Henderson?"

"Fanny, surely that is Agatha Runcible, poor Viola Chasm's daughter?"

"I wonder Viola allows her to go about like that. If she were my daughter . . ."

"*Your* daughter, Fanny . . ."

"Kitty, that was not kind."

"My dear, I only meant . . . have you, by the way, heard of her lately?"

"The last we heard was worse than anything, Kitty. She has left Buenos Aires. I am afraid she has severed her connection with Lady Metroland altogether. They think that she is in some kind of touring company."

"Darling, I'm sorry. I should never have mentioned it, but whenever I see Agatha Runcible I can't help thinking . . . girls seem to know so much nowadays. We had to learn everything for ourselves, didn't we, Fanny, and it took so long. If I'd had Agatha Runcible's chances . . . Who is the young man with her?"

"I don't know, and, frankly, I don't think, do you? . . . He has that self-contained look."

"He has very nice eyes. And he moves well."

"I dare say when it came to the point . . . Still, as I say, if I had had Agatha Runcible's advantages . . ."

"What are you looking for, darling?"

"Why, darling, such an extraordinary thing. Here *is* the sal volatile next to my brushes all the time."

"Fanny, how awful of me, if I'd only known . . ."

"I dare say there must have been another bottle you saw on the dressing-table, sweetest. Perhaps the maid put it there. You never know at the Lotti, do you?"

"Fanny, forgive me . . ."

"But, dearest, what is there to forgive? After all, you *did see* another bottle, didn't you, Kitty darling?"

"Why, look, there's Miles."

"Miles?"

"Your son, darling. My nephew, you know."

"*Miles*. Do you know, Kitty, I believe it is. He never comes to see me now, the naughty boy."

"My dear, he looks terribly *tapette*."

"Darling, I know. It is a great grief to me. Only I try not to think about it too much—he had so little chance with poor Throbbing what he was."

"The sins of the fathers, Fanny . . ."

Somewhere not far from Maidstone Mr. Outrage became fully conscious. Opposite him in the carriage the two detectives slept, their bowler hats jammed forwards on their foreheads, their mouths open, their huge red hands lying limply in their laps. Rain beat on the windows; the carriage was intensely cold and smelt of stale tobacco. Inside there were advertisements of horrible picturesque ruins; outside in the rain were hoardings advertising patent medicines and dog biscuits. "Every Molassine dog cake wags a tale."

Mr. Outrage read, and the train repeated over and over again, "Right Honourable gent, Right Honourable gent, Right Honourable gentleman, Right Honourable gent . . ."

Adam got into the carriage with the Younger Set. They still looked a bit queer, but they cheered up wonderfully when they heard about Miss Runcible's outrageous treatment at the hands of the Customs officers.

"*Well,*" they said. "*Well!* how too, too shaming, Agatha, darling," they said. "How devastating, how unpoliceman-like, how goat-like, how sick-making, how too, too awful." And then they began talking about Archie Schwert's party that night.

"Who's Archie Schwert?" asked Adam.

"Oh, he's someone new since you went away. The *most* bogus man. Miles discovered him, and since then he's been climbing and climbing and *climbing,* my dear, till he hardly knows us. He's rather sweet really, only too terribly common, poor darling. He lives at the Ritz, and I think that's rather grand, don't you?"

"Is he giving his party there?"

"My dear, of course not. In Edward Throbbing's

house. He's Miles' brother, you know, only he's frightfully dim and political, and doesn't know anybody. He got ill and went to Kenya or somewhere and left his perfectly sheepish house in Hertford Street, so we've all gone to live there. You'd better come, too. The caretakers didn't like it a bit at first, but we gave them drinks and things, and now they're simply thrilled to the marrow about it and spend all their time cutting out 'bits,' my dear, from the papers about our goings on.

"One awful thing is we haven't got a car. Miles broke it, Edward's I mean, and we simply can't afford to get it mended, so I think we shall have to move soon. Everything's getting rather broken up, too, and dirty, if you know what I mean. Because, you see, there aren't any servants only the butler and his wife and they are always tight now. So demoralizing. Mary Mouse has been a perfect angel, and sent us great hampers of caviare and things. . . . She's paying for Archie's party tonight, of course."

"Do you know, I rather think I'm going to be sick again?"

"Oh, Miles!"

(Oh, Bright Young People!)

30

Packed all together in a second-class carriage the angels were late in recovering their good humour.

"She's taken Prudence off in her car again," said Divine Discontent, who once, for one delirious fortnight, had been Mrs. Ape's favourite girl. "Can't see what she sees in her. What's London like, Fortitude? I never been there but once."

"Just exactly heaven. Shops and all."

"What are the men like, Fortitude?"

"Say, don't you never think of nothing but *men*, Chastity?"

"I should say I do. I was only asking."

"Well, they ain't much to look at, not after the shops. But they has their uses."

"Say, did you hear that? You're a cute one, Fortitude. Did you hear what Fortitude said, she said 'they have their uses.' "

"What, shops?"

"No, silly, men."

"*Men.* That's a good one, I should say."

Presently the train arrived at Victoria, and all these passengers were scattered all over London.

Adam left his bag at Shepheard's Hotel, and drove straight to Henrietta Street to see his publishers. It

31

was nearly closing time, so that most of the staff had packed up and gone home, but by good fortune Mr. Sam Benfleet, the junior director with whom Adam always did his business, was still in his room correcting proofs for one of his women novelists. He was a competent young man, with a restrained elegance of appearance (the stenographer always trembled slightly when she brought him his cup of tea).

"No, she can't print that," he kept saying, endorsing one after another of the printer's protests. "No, damn it, she can't print *that*. She'll have us all in prison." For it was one of his most exacting duties to "ginger up" the more reticent of the manuscripts submitted and "tone down" the more "outspoken" until he had reduced them all to the acceptable moral standard of his day.

He greeted Adam with the utmost cordiality.

"Well, well, Adam, how are you? This is nice. Sit down. Have a cigarette. What a day to arrive in London. Did you have a good crossing?"

"Not too good."

"I say, I *am* sorry. Nothing so beastly as a beastly crossing, is there? Why don't you come round to dinner at Wimpole Street tonight? I've got some rather nice Americans coming. Where are you staying?"

"At Shepheard's—Lottie Crump's."

"Well, that's always fun. I've been trying to get an autobiography out of Lottie for ten years. And that reminds me. You're bringing us your manuscript, aren't you? Old Rampole was asking about it only the other day. It's a week overdue, you know. I hope you've liked the preliminary notices we've sent out. We've fixed the day of publication for the second week in December, so as to give it a fortnight's run before Johnnie Hoop's autobiography. That's going to be a seller. Sails a bit near the wind in places. We had to cut out some things—you know what old Rampole is. Johnnie didn't like it a bit. But I'm looking forward terribly to reading yours."

"Well, Sam, rather an awful thing happened about that . . ."

"I say, I hope you're not going to say it's not finished. The date on the contract, you know . . ."

"Oh, it's finished all right. Burnt."

"Burnt?"

"Burnt."

"What an awful thing. I hope you are insured."

Adam explained the circumstances of the destruction of his autobiography. There was a longish pause while Sam Benfleet thought.

"What worries me is how are we going to make that sound convincing to old Rampole."

"I should think it sounded convincing enough."

"You don't know old Rampole. It's sometimes very difficult for me, Adam, working under him. Now if I had my own way I'd say, 'Take your own time. Start again. Don't worry . . .' But there's old Rampole. He's a devil for contracts, you know, and you did *say*, didn't you . . . ? It's all very difficult. You know, I wish it hadn't happened."

"So do I, oddly enough," said Adam.

"There's another difficulty. You've had an advance already, haven't you? Fifty pounds, wasn't it? Well, you know, *that* makes things very difficult. Old Rampole never likes big advances like that to young authors. You know I hate to say it, but I can't help feeling that the best thing would be for you to repay the advance—plus interest, of course, old Rampole would insist on that—and cancel the contract. Then if you ever thought of rewriting the book, well, of course, we should be delighted to consider it. I suppose that, well, I mean it *would* be quite *convenient*, and all that, to repay the advance?"

"Not only inconvenient, but impossible," said Adam in no particular manner.

34

There was another pause.

"Deuced awkward," said Sam Benfleet. "It's a shame the way the Customs House officers are allowed to take the law into their own hands. Quite ignorant men, too. Liberty of the subject, I mean, and all that. I tell you what we'll do. We'll start a correspondence about it in the *New Statesman*. . . . It is all so deuced awkward. But I think I can see a way out. I suppose you could get the book rewritten in time for the Spring List? Well, we'll cancel the contract and forget all about the advance. No, no, my dear fellow, don't thank me. If only I was alone here I'd be doing that kind of thing all day. Now instead we'll have a new contract. It won't be quite so good as the last, I'm afraid. Old Rampole wouldn't stand for that. I'll tell you what, we'll give you our standard first-novel contract. I've got a printed form here. It won't take a minute to fill up. Just sign here."

"May I just see the terms?"

"Of course, my dear fellow. They look a bit hard at first, I know, but it's our usual form. We made a very special case for you, you know. It's very simple. No royalty on the first two thousand, then a royalty of two and a half per cent., rising to five per cent. on the tenth thousand. We retain serial, cinema, dramatic, American, colonial and translation rights, of course. And, of course, an option on your next twelve books on the same terms. It's a very straightforward arrangement really. Doesn't leave room for any of the disputes which embitter the relations of author and publisher. Most of our authors are working on a contract like that. . . . Splendid. Now don't you bother any more about that advance. I understand *perfectly*, and I'll square old Rampole somehow, even if it comes out of my director's fees."

"Square old Rampole," repeated Mr. Benfleet thoughtfully as Adam went downstairs. It was fortunate, he reflected, that none of the authors ever came across the senior partner, that benign old gentleman, who once a week drove up to board meetings from the country, whose chief interest in the business was confined to the progress of a little book of his own about bee-keeping, which they had published twenty years ago and, though he did not know it, allowed long ago to drop out of print. He often wondered in his uneasy moments what he would find to say when Rampole died.

It was about now that Adam remembered that he was engaged to be married. The name of his young

36

lady was Nina Blount. So he went into a tube station to a telephone-box, which smelt rather nasty, and rang her up.

"Hullo."

"Hullo."

"May I speak to Miss Blount, please?"

"I'll just see if she's in," said Miss Blount's voice. "Who's speaking, please?" She was always rather snobbish about this fiction of having someone to answer the telephone.

"Mr. Fenwick-Symes."

"Oh."

"Adam, you know. How are you, Nina?"

"Well, I've got rather a pain just at present."

"Poor Nina. Shall I come round and see you?"

"No, don't do that, darling, because I'm just going to have a bath. Why don't we dine together?"

"Well, I asked Agatha Runcible to dinner."

"Why?"

"She'd just had all her clothes taken off by some sailors."

"Yes, I know, it's all in the evening paper tonight. . . . Well, I'll tell you what. Let's meet at Archie Schwert's party. Are you going?"

"I rather said I would."

"That's all right, then. Don't dress up. No one will, except Archie."

"Oh, I say. Nina, there's one thing—I don't think I shall be able to marry you after all."

"Oh, *Adam,* you are a bore. Why not?"

"They burnt my book."

"Beasts. Who did?"

"I'll tell you about it tonight."

"Yes, *do.* Good-bye, darling."

"Good-bye, my sweet."

He hung up the receiver and left the telephone-box. People had crowded into the Underground station for shelter from the rain, and were shaking their umbrellas and reading their evening papers. Adam could see the headlines over their shoulders.

PEER'S DAUGHTER'S DOVER ORDEAL
SERIOUS ALLEGATIONS BY SOCIETY
BEAUTY
HON. A. RUNCIBLE SAYS "TOO
SHAMING"

"Poor pretty," said an indignant old woman at his

elbow. "Disgraceful, I calls it. And such a good sweet face. I see her picture in the papers only yesterday. Nasty prying minds. That's what they got. And her poor father and all. Look, Jane, there's a piece about him, too. 'Interviewed at the Carlton Club this evening, Lord Chasm,' that's her dad, 'refused to make a definite statement. "The matter shall not be allowed to rest here," he said.' *And* quite right, too, I says. You know I feels about that girl just as though it was me own daughter. Seeing her picture so often and our Sarah having done the back stairs, Tuesdays, at them flats where her aunt used to live—the one as had that 'orrible divorce last year."

Adam bought a paper. He had just ten shillings left in the world. It was too wet to walk, so he took a very crowded tube train to Dover Street and hurried across in the rain to Shepheard's Hotel (which, for the purposes of the narrative, may be assumed to stand at the corner of Hay Hill).

III

OTTIE CRUMP, proprietress of Shepheard's Hotel, Dover Street, attended invariably by two Cairn terriers, is a happy reminder to us that the splendours of the Edwardian era were not entirely confined to Lady Anchorage or Mrs. Blackwater. She is a fine figure of a woman, singularly unscathed by any sort of misfortune and superbly oblivious of those changes in the social order which agitate the more observant *grandes dames* of her period. When the war broke out she took down the signed photograph of the Kaiser and, with some solemnity, hung it in the men-servants' lavatory; it was her one combative action; since then she has had her worries —income-tax forms and drink restrictions and young men whose fathers she used to know, who give her bad cheques, but these have been soon forgotten; one can go to Shepheard's parched with modernity any day, if Lottie likes one's face, and still draw up, cool

40

and uncontaminated, great, healing draughts from the well of Edwardian certainty.

Shepheard's has a plain, neatly pointed brick front and large, plain doorway. Inside it is like a country house. Lottie is a great one for sales, and likes, whenever one of her great houses of her day is being sold up, to take away something for old times' sake. There is a good deal too much furniture at Shepheard's, some of it rare, some of it hideous beyond description; there is plenty of red plush and red morocco and innumerable wedding presents of the 'eighties; in particular many of those massive, mechanical devices covered with crests and monograms, and associated in some way with cigars. It is the sort of house in which one expects to find croquet mallets and polo sticks in the bathroom, and children's toys at the bottom of one's chest of drawers, and an estate map and an archery target—exuding straw—and a bicycle and one of those walking-sticks which turn into saws, somewhere in passages, between baize doors, smelling of damp. (As a matter of fact, all you are likely to find in your room at Lottie's is an empty champagne bottle or two and a crumpled camisole.)

The servants, like the furniture, are old and have seen aristocratic service. Doge, the head waiter, who is hard of hearing, partially blind, and tortured with gout, was once a Rothschild's butler. He has, in fact, on more than one occasion in Father Rothschild's youth, dandled him on his knee, when he came with his father (at one time the fifteenth richest man in the world) to visit his still richer cousins, but it would be unlike him to pretend that he ever really liked the embryo Jesuit who was "too clever by half," given to asking extraordinary questions, and endowed with a penetrating acumen in the detection of falsehood and exaggeration.

Besides Doge, there are innumerable old house-maids always trotting about with cans of hot water and clean towels. There is also a young Italian who does most of the work and gets horribly insulted by Lottie, who once caught him powdering his nose, and will not let him forget it. Indeed, it is one of the few facts in Lottie's recent experience that seems always accessible.

Lottie's parlour, in which most of the life of Shep-heard's centres, contains a comprehensive collection of signed photographs. Most of the male members of the royal families of Europe are represented (except the ex-Emperor of Germany, who has not been reinstated, although there was a distinct return of sen-

42

timent towards him on the occasion of his second marriage). There are photographs of young men on horses riding in steeple-chases, of elderly men leading in the winners of "classic" races, of horses alone and of young men alone, dressed in tight white collars or in the uniform of the Brigade of Guards. There are caricatures by "Spy," and photographs cut from illustrated papers, many of them with brief obituary notices, "killed in action." There are photographs of yachts in full sail and of elderly men in yachting caps; there are some terribly funny pictures of the earliest kind of motor car. There are very few writers or painters and no actors, for Lottie is true to the sound old snobbery of pounds sterling and strawberry leaves.

Lottie was standing in the hall abusing the Italian waiter when Adam arrived.

"Well," she said, "you are a stranger. Come along in. We were just thinking about having a little drink. You'll find a lot of your friends here."

She led Adam into the parlour, where they found several men, none of whom Adam had ever seen before.

"You all know Lord Thingummy, don't you?" said Lottie.

"Mr. Symes," said Adam.

"Yes, dear, that's what I said. Bless you, I knew you before you were born. How's your father? Not dead, is he?"

"Yes, I'm afraid he is."

"Well, I never. I could tell you some things about him. Now let me introduce you—that's Mr. What's-his-name, you remember him, don't you? And over there in the corner, that's the Major, and there's Mr. What-d'you-call-him, and that's an American, and there's the King of Ruritania."

"Alas, no longer," said a sad, bearded man.

"Poor chap," said Lottie Crump, who always had a weak spot for royalty even when deposed. "It's a shame. They gave him the boot after the war. Hasn't got a penny. Not that he ever did have much. His wife's locked up in a looney house, too."

"Poor Maria Cristina. It is true how Mrs. Crump says. Her brains, they are quite gone out. All the time she thinks everyone is a bomb."

"It's perfectly true, poor old girl," said Lottie with relish. "I drove the King down Saturday to see her . . . (I won't have him travelling third class.) It fair brought tears to my eyes. Kept skipping about all the

44

time, she did, dodging. Thought they were throwing things at her."

"It is one strange thing, too," said the King. "All my family they have bombs thrown at them, but the Queen, never. My poor Uncle Joseph he blow all to bits one night at the opera, and my sister she find three bombs in her bed. But my wife, never. But one day her maid is brushing her hair before dinner, and she said, 'Madam,' she said, 'the cook has had lesson from the cook at the French Legation'—the food at my home was not what you call *chic*. One day it was mutton hot, then mutton cold, then the same mutton hot again, but less nicer, not *chic*, you understand me—'he has had lessons from the French cook,' the maid say, 'and he has made one big bomb as a surprise for your dinner-party tonight for the Swedish Minister.' Then the poor Queen say 'Oh,' like so, and since then always her poor brains has was all nohow."

The ex-King of Ruritania sighed heavily and lit a cigar.

"Well," said Lottie, brushing aside a tear, "what about a little drink? Here, you over there, your Honour Judge What's-your-name, how about a drink for the gentlemen?"

The American, who, like all the listeners, had been profoundly moved by the ex-King's recitation, roused himself to bow and say, "I shall esteem it a great honour if His Majesty and yourself, Mrs. Crump, and these other good gentlemen . . ."

"That's the way," said Lottie. "Hi, there, where's my Fairy Prince? Powdering hisself again, I suppose. Come here, Nancy, and put away the beauty cream."

In came the waiter.

"Bottle of wine," said Lottie, "with Judge Thingummy there." (Unless specified in detail, all drinks are champagne in Lottie's parlour. There is also a mysterious game played with dice which always ends with someone giving a bottle of wine to everyone in the room, but Lottie has an equitable soul and she generally sees to it, in making up the bills, that the richest people pay for everything.)

After the third or fourth bottle of wine Lottie said, "Who d'you think we've got dining upstairs tonight? *Prime Minister.*"

"Me, I have never liked Prime Ministers. They talk and talk and then they talk more. 'Sir, you must sign that.' 'Sir, you must go here and there.' 'Sir, you must do up that button before you give audience to the black plenipotentiary from Liberia.' Pah! After the

46

war my people give me the bird, yes, but they throw my Prime Minister out of the window, bump right bang on the floor. Ha, ha."

"He ain't alone either," said Lottie with a terrific wink.

"What, Sir James Brown?" said the Major, shocked in spite of himself, "I don't believe it."

"No, name of Outrage."

"He's not Prime Minister."

"Yes, he is. I saw it in the paper."

"No, he's not. He went out of office last week."

"Well I never. How they keep changing. I've no patience with it. Doge. Doge. What's the Prime Minister's name?"

"Beg pardon, mum."

"What's the name of the Prime Minister?"

"Not tonight, I don't think, mum, not as I've been informed anyway."

"What's the name of the Prime Minister, you stupid old man?"

"Oh, I beg your pardon, mum. I didn't quite hear you. Sir James Brown, mum, Bart. A very nice gentleman, so I've been told. Conservative, I've heard said. Gloucestershire they come from, I think."

"There, what did I say?" said Lottie triumphantly.

47

"It is one very extraordinary thing, your British Constitution," said the ex-King of Ruritania. "All the time when I was young they taught me nothing but British Constitution. My tutor had been a master at your Eton school. And now when I come to England always there is a different Prime Minister and no one knows which is which."

"Oh, sir," said the Major, "that's because of the Liberal Party."

"Liberals? Yes. We, too, had Liberals. I tell you something now, I had a gold fountain-pen. My god-father, the good Archduke of Austria, give me one gold fountain-pen with eagles on him. I loved my gold fountain-pen." Tears stood in the King's eyes. Champagne was a rare luxury to him now. "I loved very well my pen with the little eagles. And one day there was a Liberal minister. A Count Tampen, one man, Mrs. Crump, of exceedingly evilness. He come to talk to me and he stood at my little escritoire and he thump and talk too much about somethings I not understand, and when he go—where was my gold fountain-pen with the eagles—gone too."

"Poor old King," said Lottie. "I tell you what. You have another drink."

". . . Esteem it a great honour," said the American, "if your Majesty and these gentlemen and Mrs. Crump . . ."

"Doge, tell my little love-bird to come hopping in . . . you there, Judge wants another bottle of wine."

". . . Should honour it a great esteem . . . esteem it a great honour if Mrs. Majesty, and these gentlemen and His Crump . . ."

"That's all right, Judge. Another bottle coming."

". . . Should esteem it a great Crump if his honour and these Majesties and Mrs. Gentlemen . . ."

"Yes, yes, that's all right, Judge. Don't let him fall down, boys. Bless me, how these Americans do drink."

". . . I should Crump it a great Majesty if Mrs. Esteem . . ."

And his Honour Judge Skimp of the Federal High Court began to laugh rather a lot. (It must be remembered in all these people's favour that none of them had yet dined.)

Now there was a very bland, natty, moustachioed young man sitting there who had been drinking away quietly in the corner without talking to anyone except for an occasional "Cheerioh" to Judge Skimp. Suddenly he got up and said:

"Bet-you-can't-do-this."

49

He put three halfpennies on the table, moved them about very deliberately for a bit, and then looked up with an expression of pride. "Only touched each halfpenny five times, and changed their positions twice," he said. "Do-it-again if you like."

"Well, isn't he a clever boy?" said Lottie. "Wherever did they teach you that?"

"Chap-in-a-train showed me," he said.

"It didn't look very hard," said Adam.

"Just-you-try. Bet-you-anything-you-like you can't do it."

"How much will you bet?" Lottie loved this kind of thing.

"Anything-you-like. Five hundred pounds."

"Go on," said Lottie. "You do it. He's got lots of money."

"All right," said Adam.

He took the halfpennies and moved them about just as the young man had done. When he finished he said, "How's that?"

"Well, I'm jiggered," said the young man. "Never saw anyone do it like that before. I've won a lot of money this week with that trick. Here you are." And he took out a note-case and gave Adam a five-hundred-pound note. Then he sat down in his corner again.

"Well," said Lottie with approval, "that's sporting. Give the boys a drink for that."

So they all had another drink.

Presently the young man stood up again.

"Toss you double-or-quits," he said. "Best-out-of-three."

"All right," said Adam.

They tossed twice and Adam won both times.

"Well, I'm jiggered," said the young man, handing over another note. "You are a lucky chap."

"He's got pots of money," said Lottie. "A thousand pounds is nothing to him."

She liked to feel like that about all her guests. Actually in this young man's case she was wrong. He happened to have all that money in his pocket because he had just sold out his few remaining securities to buy a new motor car. So next day he bought a second-hand motor bicycle instead.

Adam felt a little dizzy, so he had another drink.

"D'you mind if I telephone?" he said.

He rang up Nina Blount.

"Is that Nina?"

"Adam dear, you're tight already."

"How d'you know?"

"I can hear it. What is it? I'm just going out to dinner."

"I just rang up to say that it's all right about our getting married. I've got a thousand pounds."

"Oh, good. How?"

"I'll tell you when we meet. Where are we dining?"

"Ritz. Archie. Darling, I *am* glad about our getting married."

"So am I. But don't let's get intense about it."

"I wasn't, and anyway you're tight."

He went back to the parlour. Miss Runcible had arrived and was standing in the hall very much dressed up.

"Who's that tart?" asked Lottie.

"That's not a tart, Lottie, that's Agatha Runcible."

"Looks like a tart. How do you do, my dear, come in. We're just thinking of having a little drink. You know everyone here, of course, don't you? That's the King with the beard. . . . No, deary, the King of Ruritania. You didn't mind my taking you for a tart, did you, dear? You look so like one, got up like that. Of course, I can see you aren't now."

"*My dear,*" said Miss Runcible, "if you'd seen me

52

this afternoon . . ." and she began to tell Lottie Crump about the Customs House.

"What would you do if you suddenly got a thousand pounds?" Adam asked.

"A thousand *pound*," said the King, his eyes growing dreamy at this absurd vision. "Well, first I should buy a house and a motor car and a yacht and a new pair of gloves, and then I would start one little newspaper in my country to say that I must come back and be the King, and then I don't know what I do, but I have such fun and grandness again."

"But you can't do all that with a thousand pounds, you know, sir."

"No . . . can't I not? . . . not with thousand pound. . . . Oh, well, then I think I buy a gold pen with eagles on him like the Liberals stole."

"I know what I'd do," said the Major. "I'd put it on a horse."

"What horse?"

"I can tell you a likely outsider for the November Handicap. Horse named Indian Runner. It's at twenty to one at present, and the odds are likely to lengthen. Now if you were to put a thousand on him to win and he won, why you'd be rich, wouldn't you?"

"Yes, so I would. How marvellous. D'you know, I

think I'll do that. It's a *very* good idea. How can I do it?"

"Just you give me the thousand and I'll arrange it."

"I say, that's awfully nice of you."

"Not at all."

"No, really, I think that's frightfully nice of you. Look, here's the money. Have a drink, won't you?"

"No, you have one with me."

"I said it first."

"Let's both have one, then."

"Wait a minute though, I must go and telephone about this."

He rang up the Ritz and got on to Nina.

"Darling, you do telephone a lot, don't you?"

"Nina, I've something very important to say."

"Yes, darling."

"Nina, have you heard of a horse called Indian Runner?"

"Yes, I think so. Why?"

"What sort of a horse is it?"

"My dear, quite the worst sort of horse. Mary Mouse's mother owns it."

"Not a good horse?"

"No."

"Not likely to win the November Handicap, I mean."

"Quite sure not to. I don't suppose it'll run even. Why?"

"I say, Nina, d'you know I don't think we shall be able to get married after all."

"Why not, my sweet?"

"You see, I've put my thousand pounds on Indian Runner."

"That was silly. Can't you get it back?"

"I gave it to a major."

"What sort of a major?"

"Rather a drunk one. I don't know his name."

"Well I should try and catch him. I must go back and eat now. Good-bye."

But when he got back to Lottie's parlour the Major was gone.

"What major?" said Lottie, when he asked about him. "I never saw a major."

"The one you introduced me to in the corner."

"How d'you know he's a major?"

"You said he was."

"My dear boy, I've never seen him before. Now I come to think of it, he did look like a major, didn't

55

he? But this sweet little girlie here is telling me a story. Go on, my dear. I can hardly bear to hear it, it's so wicked."

While Miss Runcible finished her story (which began to sound each time she told it more and more like the most lubricious kind of anti-Turkish propaganda) the ex-King of Ruritania told Adam about a major *he* had known, who had come from Prussia to reorganize the Ruritanian Army. He had disappeared south, taking with him all the mess plate of the Royal Guard, and the Lord Chamberlain's wife, and a valuable pair of candle-sticks from the Chapel Royal.

By the time Miss Runcible had finished, Lottie was in a high state of indignation.

"The very idea of it," she said. "The dirty hounds. And I used to know your poor father, too, before you were born *or* thought of. I'll talk to the Prime Minister about this," she said, taking up the telephone. "Give me Outrage," she said to the exchange boy. "He's up in number twelve with a Japanese."

"Outrage isn't Prime Minister, Lottie."

"Of course he is. Didn't Doge say so? . . . Hullo, is that Outrage? This is Lottie. A fine chap you are, I don't think. Tearing the clothes off the back of a poor innocent girl."

Lottie prattled on.

Mr. Outrage had finished dinner, and, as matter of fact, the phrasing of this accusation was not wholly inappropriate to his mood. It was some minutes before he began to realize that all this talk was only about Miss Runcible. By that time Lottie's flow of invective had come to an end, but she finished finely.

"Outrage your name, and Outrage your nature," she said, banging down the receiver. "And that's what I think of *him*. Now how about a little drink?"

But her party was breaking up. The Major was gone. Judge Skimp was sleeping, his fine white hair in an ash-tray. Adam and Miss Runcible were talking about where they would dine. Soon only the King remained. He gave her his arm with a grace he had acquired many years ago; far away in his sunny little palace, under a great chandelier which scattered with stars of light, like stones from a broken necklace, a crimson carpet woven with a pattern of crowned ciphers.

So Lottie and the King went in to dinner together.

Upstairs in No. 12, which is a suite of notable grandeur, Mr. Outrage was sliding back down the path of self-confidence he had so laboriously climbed.

He really would have brought matters to a crisis if it had not been for that telephone, he told himself, but now the Baroness was saying she was sure he was busy, must be wanting her to go: would he order her car.

It was so difficult. For a European the implications of an invitation to dinner *tête-à-tête* in a private room at Shepheard's were definitively clear. Her acceptance on the first night of his return to England had thrown him into a flutter of expectation. But all through dinner she had been so self-possessed, so supremely social. Yet, surely, just before the telephone rang, surely then, when they left the table and moved to the fire, there had been *something* in the atmosphere. But you never knew with Orientals. He clutched his knees and said in a voice which sounded very extraordinary to him, must she go, it was lovely after a fortnight, and then, desperately, he had thought of her in Paris such a lot. (Oh, for words, words! That massed treasury of speech that was his to squander at will, to send bowling and spinning in golden pieces over the floor of the House of Commons; that glorious largesse of vocables he cast far and wide, in ringing handfuls about his constituency!)

The little Baroness Yoshiwara, her golden hands

clasped in the lap of her golden Paquin frock, sat where she had been sent, more puzzled than Mr. Outrage, waiting for orders. What did the clever Englishman want? If he was busy with his telephone, why did he not send her away; tell her another time to come: if he wanted to be loved, why did he not tell her to come over to him? Why did he not pick her out of her red plush chair and sit her on his knee? Was she, perhaps, looking ugly tonight? She had thought not. It was so hard to know what these Occidentals wanted.

Then the telephone rang again.

"Will you hold on a minute? Father Rothschild wants to speak to you," said a voice. ". . . Is that you, Outrage? Will you be good enough to come round and see me as soon as you can? There are several things which I must discuss with you."

"Really, Rothschild . . . I don't see why I should. I have a guest."

"The Baroness had better return immediately. The waiter who brought you your coffee has a brother at the Japanese Embassy."

"Good God, has he? But why don't you go and worry Brown? He's P.M., you know, not me."

"You will be in office tomorrow. . . . As soon as possible, please, at my usual address."

"Oh, all right."

"Why, of course."

IV

T Archie Schwert's party the fifteenth Marquess of Vanburgh, Earl Vanburgh de Brendon, Baron Brendon, Lord of the Five Isles and Hereditary Grand Falconer to the Kingdom of Connaught, said to the eighth Earl of Balcairn, Viscount Erdinge, Baron Cairn of Balcairn, Red Knight of Lancaster, Count of the Holy Roman Empire and Chenonceaux Herald to the Duchy of Aquitaine, "Hullo," he said. "Isn't this a repulsive party? What are you going to say about it?" for they were both of them, as it happened, gossip writers for the daily papers.

"I've just telephoned my story through," said Lord Balcairn. "And now I'm going, thank God."

"I can't think of what to say," said Lord Vanburgh. "My editress said yesterday she was tired of seeing the same names over and over again—and here they

61

are again, all of them. There's Nina Blount's engagement being broken off, but she's not got any publicity value to speak of. Agatha Runcible's usually worth a couple of paragraphs, but they're featuring her as a front-page news story tomorrow over this Customs House business."

"I made rather a good thing over Edward Throbbing being in a log shanty in Canada which he built himself with the help of one Red Indian. I thought that was fairly good because you see I could contrast that with Miles being dressed as a Red Indian tonight, don't you think so, or don't you?"

"I say, that's rather good, may I use it?"

"Well, you can have the shanty, but the Red Indian's mine."

"Where is he actually?"

"Heaven knows. Government House at Ottawa, I think."

"Who's that awful-looking woman? I'm sure she's famous in some way. It's not Mrs. Melrose Ape, is it? I heard she was coming."

"Who?"

"That one. Making up to Nina."

"Good lord, no. She's no one. Mrs. Panrast she's called now."

"She seems to know you."

"Yes, I've known her all my life. As a matter of fact, she's my mother."

"My dear, how too shaming. D'you mind if I put that in?"

"I'd sooner you didn't. The family can't bear her. She's been divorced twice since then, you know."

"My dear, of course not, I quite understand."

Five minutes later he was busy at the telephone, dictating his story. ". . . Orchid stop, new paragraph. One of the most striking women in the room was Mrs. Panrast—P-A-N-R-A-S-T, no T for telephone, you know—formerly Countess of Balcairn. She dresses with that severely masculine chic, italics, which American women know so well how to assume, stop. Her son, comma, the present Earl, comma, was with her, stop. Lord Balcairn is one of the few young men about town . . .

". . . the Hon. Miles Malpractice was dressed as a Red Indian. He is at present living in the house of his brother, Lord Throbbing, at which yesterday's party was held. His choice of costume was particularly— what shall I say, hullo, yes—was particularly piquant, italics, since the latest reports of Lord Throbbing say that he is living in a log shack in Canada which he built with his own hands, aided by one Red Indian servant, stop. . . ."

You see that was the kind of party Archie Schwert's party was.

Miss Mouse (in a very enterprising frock by Cheruit) sat on a chair with her eyes popping out of her head. She never *could* get used to so much excitement, never. Tonight she had brought a little friend with her—a Miss Brown—because it was so much more fun if one had someone to talk to. It was too thrilling to see all that dull money her father had amassed, metamorphosed in this way into so much glitter and noise and so many bored young faces. Archie Schwert, as he passed, champagne bottle in hand, paused to say, "How are you, Mary darling? Quite all right?"

"That's Archie Schwert," said Miss Mouse to Miss Brown. "Isn't he too clever?"

"Is he?" said Miss Brown, who would have liked a drink, but didn't know how quite to set about it. "You *are* lucky to know such amusing people, Mary darling. I never see anyone."

"Wasn't the invitation clever? Johnnie Hoop wrote it."

64

"Well, yes, I suppose it was. But you know (was it dreadful of me?) I hadn't heard of any of the names."*

"My dear, of course you have," said Miss Mouse, feeling somewhere in her depths—those unplumbed places in Miss Mouse's soul—a tiny, most unaccustomed flicker of superiority; for she had gone through that invitation word by word in papa's library some days ago and knew all about it.

She almost wished in this new mood of exaltation that she had come to the party in fancy dress. It was called a Savage party, that is to say that Johnnie Hoop had written on the invitation that they were to come dressed as savages. Numbers of them had done so; Johnnie himself in a mask and black gloves represented the Maharanee of Pukkapore, somewhat

* Perhaps it should be explained—there were at this time three sorts of formal invitation card; there was the nice sensible copybook hand sort with a name and *At Home* and a date and time and address; then there was the sort that came from Chelsea, *Noel and Audrey are having a little whoopee on Saturday evening: do please come and bring a bottle too, if you can;* and finally there was the sort that Johnnie Hoop used to adapt from *Blast* and Marinetti's *Futurist Manifesto*. These had two columns of close print; in one was a list of all the things Johnnie hated, and in the other all the things he thought he liked. Most of the parties which Miss Mouse financed had invitations written by Johnnie Hoop.

to the annoyance of the Maharajah, who happened to drop in. The real aristocracy, the younger members of those two or three great brewing families which rule London, had done nothing about it. They had come on from a dance and stood in a little group by themselves, aloof, amused but not amusing. Pit-a-pat went the heart of Miss Mouse. How she longed to tear down her dazzling frock to her hips and dance like a Bacchante before them all. One day she would surprise them all, thought Miss Mouse.

There was a famous actor making jokes (but it was not so much what he said as the way he said it that made the people laugh who did laugh). "I've come to the party as a wild widower," he said. They were that kind of joke—but, of course, he made a droll face when he said it.

Miss Runcible had changed into Hawaiian costume and was the life and soul of the evening.

She had heard someone say something about an Independent Labour Party, and was furious that she had not been asked.

There were two men with a lot of explosive powder taking photographs in another room. Their flashes and bangs had rather a disquieting effect on the party, causing a feeling of tension, because everyone looked negligent and said what a bore the papers were, and how *too* like Archie to let the photographers come, but most of them, as a matter of fact, wanted dreadfully to be photographed and the others were frozen with unaffected terror that they might be taken unawares and then their mammas would know where they had been when they said they were at the Bicesters' dance, and then there would be a row again, which was so *exhausting,* if nothing else.

There were Adam and Nina getting rather sentimental.

"D'you know," she said, pulling out a lump, "I'd quite made up my mind that your hair was dark." Archie Schwert, pausing with a bottle of champagne, said, "Don't be so sadistic, Nina."

"Go away, hog's rump," said Adam, in Cockney, adding, in softer tones, "Are you disappointed?"

"Well, no, but it's rather disconcerting getting engaged to someone with dark hair and finding it's fair."

"Anyway, we aren't engaged any more, are we— or are we?"

"I'm not sure that we're not. How much money *have* you, Adam?"

"Literally, none, my dear. Poor Agatha had to pay for dinner as it was, and God knows what I'm going to do about Lottie Crump's bill."

"Of course, you know—Adam, don't fall asleep—there's always papa. I believe he's really much richer than he looks. He might give us some money until your books start paying."

"You know, if I wrote a book a month I should be free of that contract in a year. . . . I hadn't thought of that before. I don't at all see why I shouldn't do that, do you? . . . or do you?"

"Of course not, darling. I'll tell you what. We'll go down and see papa tomorrow, shall we?"

"Yes, that would be divine, darling."

"Adam, don't go to sleep."

"Sorry, darling, what I meant was that that would be divine."

And he went to sleep for a little, with his head in her lap.

"Pretty as a picture," said Archie, in Cockney, passing with a bottle of champagne in his hand.

"Wake up, Adam," said Nina, pulling out more hair. "It's time to go."

"That would be divine. . . . I say, have I been asleep?"

"Yes, for hours and hours. You looked rather sweet."

"And you sat there. . . . I say, Nina, you are getting sentimental. . . . Where are we going?"

There were about a dozen people left at the party; that hard kernel of gaiety that never breaks. It was about three o'clock.

"Let's go to Lottie Crump's and have a drink," said Adam.

So they all got into two taxicabs and drove across Berkeley Square—which looked less than Arlenish in the rain—to Dover Street. But at Shepheard's the night porter said that Mrs. Crump had just gone to bed. He thought that Judge Skimp was still up with some friends; would they like to join them? They went up to Judge Skimp's suite, but there had been a disaster there with a chandelier that one of his young ladies had tried to swing on. They were bathing her forehead with champagne; two of them were asleep.

So Adam's party went out again into the rain.

"Of course, there's always the Ritz," said Archie.

"I believe the night porter can usually get one a drink." But he said it in the sort of voice that made all the others say, no, the Ritz was too, too boring at that time of night.

They went to Agatha Runcible's house, which was quite near, but she found that she'd lost her latch-key, so that was no good. Soon someone would say the fatal words, "Well, I think it's time for me to go to bed. Can I give anyone a lift to Knightsbridge?" and the party would be over.

But instead a little breathless voice said, "Why don't you come to *my* house?"

It was Miss Brown.

So they all got into taxicabs again and drove rather a long way to Miss Brown's house. She turned on the lights in a sombre dining-room and gave them glasses of whisky and soda. (She turned out to be rather a good hostess, though over-zealous.) Then Miles said he wanted something to eat, so they all went down-stairs into a huge kitchen lined with every shape of pot and pan and found some eggs and some bacon and Miss Brown cooked them. Then they had some more whisky upstairs and Adam fell asleep again. Pres-ently Vanburgh said, "D'you mind if I use the tele-phone? I must just send the rest of my story to the paper." Miss Brown took him to a study that looked almost like an office, and he dictated the rest of his column, and then he came back and had some more whisky.

It was a lovely evening for Miss Brown. Flushed with successful hospitality she trotted from guest to guest, offering here a box of matches, there a cigar, there a fruit from the enormous gilt dishes on the sideboard. To think that all these brilliant people, whom she had heard so much about, with what envy, from Miss Mouse, should be here in papa's dining-room, calling her "my dear" and "darling." And when at last they said they really had to go, Miss Runcible said, "Well, *I* can't go, because I've lost my latch-key. D'you mind awfully if I sleep here?"

Miss Brown, her heart in her mouth, but in the most natural way possible, said, "Of course not, Agatha darling, that would be divine."

And then Miss Runcible said, "How too divine of you, darling."

Rapture!

At half-past nine the next morning the Brown family came down to breakfast in the dining-room.

There were four quiet girls (of whom the Miss

Brown who had given the party was the youngest); their brother worked in a motor shop and had had to get off early. They were seated at the table when their mamma came down.

"Now, children," she said, "do try to remember to talk to your father at breakfast. He was quite hurt yesterday. He feels out of things. It's so easy to bring him into the conversation if you take a little trouble, and he does so enjoy hearing about everything."

"Yes, Mamma," they said. "We do try, you know."

"And what was the Bicesters' dance like, Jane?" she said, pouring out some coffee. "Did you have a good time?"

"It was just too divine," said the youngest Miss Brown.

"It was *what*, Jane?"

"I mean it was *lovely*, Mamma."

"So I should think. You girls are very lucky nowadays. There were not nearly so many dances when I was your age. Perhaps two a week in the season, you know, but *none* before Christmas ever."

"Mamma."

"Yes, Jane."

"Mamma. I asked a girl to stay the night."

"Yes, dear. When? We're rather full up, you know."

72

"Last night, Mamma."

"What an extraordinary thing to do. Did she accept?"

"Yes, she's here now."

"*Well.* . . . Ambrose, will you tell Mrs. Sparrow to put on another egg?"

"I'm very sorry, my lady, Mrs. Sparrow can't understand it, but there *are* no eggs this morning. She thinks there must have been burglars."

"Nonsense, Ambrose, who ever heard of burglars coming into a house to steal eggs?"

"The shells were all over the floor, my lady."

"I see. That's all, thank you, Ambrose. Well, Jane, has your guest eaten all our eggs too?"

"Well, I'm afraid she has . . . at least . . . I mean . . ."

At this moment Agatha Runcible came down to breakfast. She was not looking her best really in the morning light.

"Good morning all," she said in Cockney. "I've found the right room at last. D'you know, I popped into a study or something. There was a sweet old boy sitting at a desk. He *did* look surprised to see me. Was it your papa?"

"This is mamma," said Jane.

"How are you?" said Miss Runcible. "I say, I think it's quite too sweet of you to let me come down to breakfast like this." (It must be remembered that she was still in Hawaiian costume.) "Are you sure you're not *furious* with me? All this is really much more embarrassing for *me*, isn't it, don't you think . . . or don't you?"

"Do you take tea or coffee?" at last Jane's mother managed to say. "Jane, dear, give your friend some breakfast." For in the course of a long public life she had formed the opinion that a judicious offer of food eased most social situations.

Then Jane's father came in.

"Martha, the most extraordinary thing! . . . I think I must be losing my reason. I was in my study just now going over that speech for this afternoon, when suddenly the door opened and in came a sort of dancing Hottentot woman half-naked. It just said, 'Oh, how shy-making,' and then disappeared, and . . . oh . . ." For he had suddenly caught sight of Miss Runcible ". . . oh . . . how do you do? . . . How . . ."

"I don't think you have met my husband before."

"Only for a second," said Miss Runcible.

"I hope you slept well," said Jane's father desperately. "Martha never told me we had a guest. Forgive me if I appeared inhospitable . . . I—er . . . Oh, why doesn't somebody else say something."

Miss Runcible, too, was feeling the strain. She picked up the morning paper.

"Here's something terribly funny," she said, by way of making conversation. "Shall I read it to you?

"*'Midnight Orgies at No.* 10.' My dear, isn't that divine. Listen, *'What must be the most extraordinary party of the little season took place in the small hours of this morning at No.* 10, *Downing Street. At about* 4 A. M. *the policemen who are always posted outside the Prime Minister's residence were surprised to witness*—' Isn't this too amusing?—'*the arrival of a fleet of taxis, from which emerged a gay throng in exotic fancy dress'*—How I should have loved to have seen it. Can't you imagine what they were like—'*The hostess of what was described by one of the guests as the brightest party the Bright Young People have yet given, was no other than Miss Jane Brown, the youngest of the Prime Minister's four lovely daughters. The Honourable Agatha . . .'* Why, what an extraordinary thing. . . . Oh, my God!"

Suddenly light came flooding in on Miss Runcible's mind as once when, in her débutante days, she had

75

gone behind the scenes at a charity matinée, and returning had stepped through the wrong door and found herself in a blaze of flood-lights on the stage in the middle of the last act of Othello. "Oh, my God!" she said, looking round the Brown breakfast table. "Isn't that just too bad of Vanburgh. He's always doing that kind of thing. It really would serve him right if we complained and he lost his job, don't you think so, Sir James . . . or . . . don't you?"

Miss Runcible paused and met the eyes of the Brown family once more.

"Oh, dear," she said, "this really is all too bogus."

Then she turned round and trailing garlands of equatorial flowers fled out of the room and out of the house to the huge delight and profit of the crowd of reporters and Press photographers who were already massed round the historic front door.

V

DAM woke up feeling terribly ill. He rang his bell once or twice, but nobody came. Later he woke up again and rang the bell. The Italian waiter appeared, undulating slightly in the doorway. Adam ordered breakfast. Lottie came in and sat on his bed.

"Had a nice breakfast, dear?" she said.

"Not yet," said Adam, "I've only just woken up."

"That's right," said Lottie. "Nothing like a nice breakfast. There was a young lady for you on the 'phone, but I can't remember what it was she said at the minute. We've all been upside down this morning. Such a fuss. Had the police in we have, ever since I don't know what time, drinking up my wine and asking questions and putting their noses where they're not wanted. All because Flossie must needs go and swing on the chandelier. She never had any sense,

77

Flossie. Well, she's learned her lesson now, poor girl. Whoever heard of such a thing—swinging on a chandelier. Poor Judge What's-his-name is in a terrible state about it. I said to him it's not so much the price of the chandelier, I said. What money can make money can mend, I said, and that's the truth, isn't it, dear? But what I mind, I said, is having a death in the house and all the fuss. It doesn't do *anyone* any good having people killing theirselves in a house like Flossie did. Now what may *you* want, my Italian queen?" said Lottie as the waiter came in with a tray, the smell of kippers contending with *nuit de Noel* rather disagreeably.

"Gentleman's breakfast," said the waiter.

"And how many *more* breakfasts do you think he wants, I should like to know. He's had his breakfast hours ago while you were powdering your nose downstairs, haven't you, dear?"

"No," said Adam, "as a matter of fact, no."

"There, do you hear what the gentleman says? *He* doesn't want two breakfasts. Don't stand there wiggling your behind at me. Take it away quick, or I'll catch you such a smack. . . . That's just the way— once you get the police in, everyone gets all upset. There's that boy brings you two breakfasts, and I

78

dare say there's some poor fellow along the passage somewhere who hasn't had any breakfast at all. You can't get anywhere without a nice breakfast. Half the young fellows as come here now don't have anything except a *cachet Faivre* and some orange juice. It's not right," said Lottie, "and I've spoken to that boy about using scent twenty times if I've spoken once."

The waiter's head appeared, and with it another wave of *nuit de Noel*.

"If you please, madam, the inspectors want to speak to you downstairs, madam."

"All right, my little bird of paradise, I'll be there."

Lottie trotted away and the waiter came sidling back bearing his tray of kippers and leering at Adam with a horrible intimacy.

"Turn on my bath, will you, please," said Adam.

"Alas, signor, there is a gentleman asleep in the bath. Shall I wake him?"

"No, it doesn't matter."

"Will that be all, sir?"

"Yes, thank you."

The waiter stood about fingering the brass knobs at the end of the bed, smiling ingratiatingly. Then he produced from under his coat a gardenia, slightly browned at the edges. (He had found it in an evening coat he had just been brushing.)

Would the signor perhaps like a buttonhole. . . . Madame Crump was so severe . . . it was nice sometime to be able to have a talk with the gentleman . . .

"No," said Adam. "Go away." For he had a headache.

The waiter sighed deeply, and walked with pettish steps to the door; sighed again and took the gardenia to the gentleman in the bathroom.

Adam ate some breakfast. No kipper, he reflected, is ever as good as it smells; how this too earthly contact with flesh and bone spoiled the first happy exhilaration; if only one could live, as Jehovah was said to have done, on the savour of burnt offerings. He lay back for a little in his bed thinking about the smells of food, of the greasy horror of fried fish and the deeply moving smell that came from it; of the intoxicating breath of bakeries and the dullness of buns. . . . He planned dinners of enchanting aromatic foods that should be carried under the nose, snuffed and thrown to the dogs . . . endless dinners, in which one could alternate flavour with flavour from sunset to dawn without satiety, while one breathed great draughts of the bouquet of old brandy.

80

. . . Oh for the wings of a dove, thought Adam, wandering a little from the point as he fell asleep again (everyone is liable to this ninetyish feeling in the early morning after a party).

Presently the telephone by Adam's bed began ringing.

"Hullo, yes."

"Lady to speak to you. . . . Hullo, is that you, Adam?"

"Is that Nina?"

"How are you, my darling?"

"Oh, Nina. . . ."

"My poor sweet, I feel like that, too. Listen, angel. You haven't forgotten that you're going to see my papa today, have you . . . or have you? I've just sent him a wire to say that you're going to lunch with him. D'you know where he lives?"

"But you're coming too?"

"Well, no. I don't think I will, if you don't mind. . . . I've got rather a pain."

"My dear, if you *knew* what a pain I've got. . . ."

"Yes, but that's different, darling. Anyway, there's no object in our both going."

"But what am I to say?"

"*Darling*, don't be tiresome. You know perfectly well. Just ask him for some money."

"Will he like that?"

"Yes, darling, of course he will. Why will you **go** *on?* I've got to get up now. Good-bye. Take care of yourself. . . . Ring me up when you get back and tell me what papa said. By the way, have you seen the paper this morning?—there's something so funny about last night. *Too* bad of Van. Good-bye."

While Adam was dressing, he realized that he did not know where he was to go. He rang up again. "By the way, Nina, where does your papa live?"

"Didn't I tell you? It's a house called Doubting, and it's all falling down really. You go to Aylesbury by train and then take a taxi. They're the most expensive taxis in the world, too. . . . Have you got any money?"

Adam looked on the dressing-table: "About seven shillings," he said.

"My dear, that's not enough. You'll have to make poor papa pay for the taxi."

"Will he like that?"

"Yes, of course, he's an angel."

"I wish you'd come too, Nina."

"Darling, I told you. I've got such a pain."

Downstairs, as Lottie had said, everything was up-side down. That is to say that there were policemen and reporters teeming in every corner of the hotel, each with a bottle of champagne and a glass. Lottie, Doge, Judge Skimp, the Inspector, four plain-clothes men and the body were in Judge Skimp's suite.

"What is *not* clear to me, sir," said the Inspector, "is what *prompted* the young lady to swing on the chandelier. Not wishing to cause offence, sir, and begging your pardon, was she . . . ?"

"Yes," said Judge Skimp, "she was."

"*Exactly,*" said the Inspector. "A clear case of misadventure, eh, Mrs. Crump? There'll have to be an inquest, of course, but I think probably I shall be able to arrange things so that there is no mention of your name in the case, sir . . . well, that's very kind of you, Mrs. Crump, perhaps just one more glass."

"Lottie," said Adam, "can you lend me some money?"

"Money, dear? Of course. Doge, have you got any money?"

"I was asleep at the time myself, mum, and was not even made aware of the occurrence until I was called this morning. Being slightly deaf, the sound of the disaster . . ."

83

"Judge What's-your-name, got any money?"

"I should take it as a great privilege if I could be of any assistance . . ."

"That's right, give some to young Thingummy here. That all you want, deary? Don't run away. We're just thinking of having a little drink. . . . No, not that wine, dear, it's what we keep for the police. I've just ordered a better bottle if my young butterfly would bring it along."

Adam had a glass of champagne, hoping it would make him feel a little better. It made him feel much worse.

Then he went to Marylebone. It was Armistice Day, and they were selling artificial poppies in the streets. As he reached the station it struck eleven and for two minutes all over the country everyone was quiet and serious. Then he went to Aylesbury, reading on the way Balcairn's account of Archie Schwert's party. He was pleased to see himself described as "the brilliant young novelist," and wondered whether Nina's papa read gossip paragraphs, and supposed not. The two women opposite him in the carriage obviously did.

"I no sooner opened the paper," said one, "than I

was on the 'phone *at once* to all the ladies of the committee, and we'd sent off a wire to our Member before one o'clock. We know how to make things hum at the Bois. I've got a copy of what we sent. Look. *Members of the Committee of the Ladies' Conservative Association at Chesham Bois wish to express their extreme displeasure at reports in this morning's paper of midnight party at No.* 10. *They call upon Captain Crutwell*—that's our Member; such a nice stamp of man —*strenuously to withhold support to Prime Minister.* It cost nearly four shillings, but, as I said at the time, it was not a moment to spoil the ship for a ha'p'orth of tar. Don't you agree, Mrs. Ithewaite?"

"I do, indeed, Mrs. Orraway-Smith. It is clearly a case in which a mandate from the constituencies is required. I'll talk to our chairwoman at Wendover."

"Yes, do, Mrs. Ithewaite. It is in a case like this that the woman's vote can count."

"If it's a choice between my moral judgment and the nationalization of banking, I prefer nationalization, if you see what I mean."

"Exactly what I think. Such a terrible example to the lower classes, *apart from everything.*"

"That's what I mean. There's our Agnes, now.

How can I stop her having young men in the kitchen when she knows that Sir James Brown has parties like that at all hours of the night. . . ."

They were both wearing hats like nothing on earth, which bobbed and nodded as they spoke.

At Aylesbury Adam got into a Ford taxi and asked to be taken to a house called Doubting.

"Doubting 'All?"

"Well I suppose so. Is it falling down?"

"Could do with a lick of paint," said the driver, a spotty youth. "Name of Blount."

"That's it."

"Long way from here, Doubting 'All is. Cost you fifteen bob."

"All right."

"If you're a commercial, I can tell you straight it ain't no use going to 'im. Young feller asked me the way there this morning. Driving a Morris. Wanted to sell him a vacuum cleaner. Old boy 'ad answered an advertisement asking for a demonstration. When he got there the old boy wouldn't even look at it. Can you beat that?"

"No, I'm not trying to sell him anything—at least not exactly."

"Personal visit, perhaps."

"Yes."

"Ah."

Satisfied that his passenger was in earnest about the journey, the taxi-driver put on some coats—for it was raining—got out of his seat and cranked up the engine. Presently they started.

They drove for a mile or two past bungalows and villas and timbered public houses to a village in which every house seemed to be a garage and filling station. Here they left the main road and Adam's discomfort became acute.

At last they came to twin octagonal lodges and some heraldic gate-posts and large wrought-iron gates, behind which could be seen a broad sweep of ill-kept drive.

"Doubting 'All," said the driver.

He blew his horn once or twice, but no lodge-keeper's wife, aproned and apple-cheeked, appeared to bob them in. He got out and shook the gates reproachfully.

"Chained-and-locked," he said. "Try another way."

They drove on for another mile; on the side of the Hall the road was bordered by dripping trees and a dilapidated stone wall; presently they reached some cottages and a white gate. This they opened and turned into a rough track, separated from the park by low iron railings. There were sheep grazing on either side. One of them had strayed into the drive. It fled before them in a frenzied trot, stopping and looking round over its dirty tail and then plunging on again until its agitation brought it to the side of the path, where they overtook it and passed it.

The tracks led to some stables, then behind rows of hothouses, among potting-sheds and heaps of drenched leaves, past nondescript outbuildings that had once been laundry and bakery and brew-house, and a huge kennel where once someone had kept a bear, until suddenly it turned by a clump of holly and elms and laurel bushes into an open space that had once been laid with gravel. A lofty Palladian façade stretched before them and in front of it an equestrian statue pointed a baton imperiously down the main drive.

" 'Ere y'are," said the driver.

Adam paid him and went up the steps to the front door. He rang the bell and waited. Nothing happened. Presently he rang again. At this moment the door opened.

"Don't ring twice," said a very angry old man, "What do you want?"

"Is Mr. Blount in?"

"There's no Mr. Blount here. This is Colonel Blount's house."

"I'm sorry. . . . I think the Colonel is expecting me to luncheon."

"Nonsense. I'm Colonel Blount," and he shut the door.

The Ford had disappeared. It was still raining hard. Adam rang again.

"Yes," said Colonel Blount, appearing instantly.

"I wonder if you'd let me telephone to the station for a taxi?"

"Not on the telephone. . . . It's raining. Why don't you come in? It's absurd to walk to the station in this. Have you come about the vacuum cleaner?"

"No."

"Funny, I've been expecting a man all the morning to show me a vacuum cleaner. Come in, do. Won't you stay to luncheon?"

"I should love to."

"Splendid. I get very little company nowadays. You must forgive me for opening the door to you myself. My butler is in bed today. He suffers terribly in his feet when it is wet. Both my footmen were killed in the war. . . . Put your hat and coat here. I hope you haven't got wet. . . . I'm sorry you didn't bring the vacuum cleaner . . . but never mind. How are you?" he said, suddenly holding out his hand.

They shook hands and Colonel Blount led the way down a long corridor, lined with marble busts on yellow marble pedestals, to a large room full of furniture, with a fire burning in a fine rococo fireplace. There was a large leather-topped walnut writing-table under a window opening on to a terrace. Colonel Blount picked up a telegram and read it.

"I'd quite forgotten," he said in some confusion. "I'm afraid you'll think me very discourteous, but it is, after all, impossible for me to ask you to luncheon. I have a guest coming on very intimate family business. You understand, don't you? . . . To tell you the truth, it's some young rascal who wants to marry my daughter. I must see him alone to discuss settlements."

"Well, I want to marry your daughter, too," said Adam.

"What an extraordinary coincidence. Are you sure you do?"

"Perhaps the telegram may be about me. What does it say?"

"'Engaged to marry Adam Symes. Expect him luncheon. Nina.' Are you Adam Symes?"

"Yes."

"My dear boy, why didn't you say so before, instead of going on about a vacuum cleaner? How are you?"

They shook hands again.

"If you don't mind," said Colonel Blount, "we will keep our business until after luncheon. I'm afraid everything is looking very bare at present. You must come down and see the gardens in the summer. We had some lovely hydrangeas last year. I don't think I shall live here another winter. Too big for an old man. I was looking at some of the houses they're putting up outside Aylesbury. Did you see them coming along? Nice little red houses. Bathroom and everything. Quite cheap, too, and near the cinematographs. I hope you are fond of the cinematograph too? The Rector and I go a great deal. I hope you'll like the Rector. Common little man rather. But he's got a motor car, useful that. How long are you staying?"

"I promised Nina I'd be back tonight."

"That's a pity. They change the film at the Electra Palace. We might have gone."

An elderly woman servant came in to announce luncheon. "What is at the Electra Palace, do you know, Mrs. Florin?"

"Greta Garbo in 'Venetian Kisses,' I think, sir."

"I don't really think I like Greta Garbo. I've tried to," said Colonel Blount, "but I just don't."

They went in to luncheon in a huge dining-room dark with family portraits.

"If you don't mind," said Colonel Blount, "I prefer not to talk at meals."

He propped a morocco-bound volume of *Punch* before his plate against a vast silver urn, from which grew a small castor-oil plant.

"Give Mr. Symes a book," he said.

Mrs. Florin put another volume of *Punch* beside Adam.

"If you come across anything really funny read it to me," said Colonel Blount.

Then they had luncheon.

They were nearly an hour over luncheon. Course followed course in disconcerting abundance while Colonel Blount ate and ate, turning the leaves of his

92

book and chuckling frequently. They ate hare soup and boiled turbot and stewed sweetbreads and black Bradenham ham with Madeira sauce and roast pheasant and a rum omelette and toasted cheese and fruit. First they drank sherry, then claret, then port. Then Colonel Blount shut his book with a broad sweep of his arm rather as the headmaster of Adam's private school used to shut the Bible after evening prayers, folded his napkin carefully and stuffed it into a massive silver ring, muttered some words of grace and finally stood up, saying:

"Well, I don't know about you, but I'm going to have a little nap," and trotted out of the room.

"There's a fire in the library, sir," said Mrs. Florin. "I'll bring you your coffee there. The Colonel doesn't have coffee, he finds it interferes with his afternoon sleep. What time would you like your afternoon tea, sir?"

"I ought really to be getting back to London. How long will it be before the Colonel comes down, do you think?"

"Well, it all depends, sir. Not usually till about five or half-past. Then he reads until dinner at seven and after dinner gets the Rector to drive him in to the pictures. A sedentary life, as you might say."

She led Adam into the library and put a silver coffee-pot at his elbow.

"I'll bring you tea at four," she said.

Adam sat in front of the fire in a deep armchair. Outside the rain beat on the double windows. There were several magazines in the library—mostly cheap weeklies devoted to the cinema. There was a stuffed owl and a case of early British remains, bone pins and bits of pottery and a skull, which had been dug up in the park many years ago and catalogued by Nina's governess. There was a cabinet containing the relics of Nina's various collecting fevers—some butterflies and a beetle or two, some fossils and some birds' eggs and a few postage stamps. There were some bookcases of superbly unreadable books, a gun, a butterfly net, an alpenstock in the corner. There were catalogues of agricultural machines and acetylene plants, lawn mowers, "sport requisites." There was a fire screen worked with a coat of arms. The chimney-piece was hung with the embroidered saddle-cloths of Colonel Blount's regiment of Lancers. There was an engraving of all the members of the Royal Yacht Squadron, with a little plan in the corner, marked to show who was who. There were many other things of equal interest besides, but before Adam had noticed any more he was fast asleep.

Mrs. Florin woke him at four. The coffee had disappeared and its place was taken by a silver tray with a lace cloth on it. There was a silver tea-pot, and a silver kettle with a little spirit-lamp underneath, and a silver cream jug and a covered silver dish full of muffins. There was also hot buttered toast and honey and gentleman's relish and a chocolate cake, a cherry cake, a seed cake and a fruit cake and some tomato sandwiches and pepper and salt and currant bread and butter.

"Would you care for a lightly boiled egg, sir? The Colonel generally has one if he's awake."

"No, thank you," said Adam. He felt a thousand times better for his rest. When Nina and he were married, he thought, they would often come down there for the day after a really serious party. For the first time he noticed an obese liver and white spaniel, which was waking up, too, on the hearthrug.

"Please not to give her muffins," said Mrs. Florin, "it's the one thing she's not supposed to have, and the Colonel will give them to her. He loves that dog," she added with a burst of confidence. "Takes her to the pictures with him of an evening. Not that she can appreciate them really like a human can."

Adam gave her—the spaniel, not Mrs. Florin—a gentle prod with his foot and a lump of sugar. She licked his shoe with evident cordiality. Adam was not above feeling flattered by friendliness in dogs.

He had finished his tea and was filling his pipe when Colonel Blount came into the library.

"Who the devil are you?" said his host.

"Adam Symes," said Adam.

"Never heard of you. How did you get in? Who gave you tea? What do you want?"

"You asked me to luncheon," said Adam. "I came about being married to Nina."

"My dear boy, of course. How absurd of me. I've such a bad memory for names. It comes of seeing so few people. How are you?"

They shook hands again.

"So you're the young man who's engaged to Nina," said the Colonel, eyeing him for the first time in the way prospective sons-in-law are supposed to be eyed. "Now what in the world do you want to get married for? I shouldn't, you know, really I shouldn't. Are you rich?"

"No, not at present, I'm afraid; that's rather what I wanted to talk about."

"How much money have you got?"

"Well, sir, actually at the moment I haven't got any at all."

"When did you last have any?"

"I had a thousand pounds last night, but I gave it all to a drunk major."

"Why did you do that?"

"Well, I hoped he'd put it on Indian Runner for the November Handicap."

"Never heard of the horse. Didn't he?"

"I don't think he can have."

"When will you next have some money?"

"When I've written some books."

"How many books?"

"Twelve."

"How much will you have then?"

"Probably fifty pounds advance on my thirteenth book."

"And how long will it take you to write twelve books?"

"About a year."

"How long would it take most people?"

"About twenty years. Of course, put like that I do

see that it sounds rather hopeless . . . but, you see, Nina and I hoped that you, that is, that perhaps for the next year until I get my twelve books written, that you might help us . . ."

"How could I help you? I've never written a book in my life."

"No, we thought you might give us some money."

"You thought that, did you?"

"Yes, that's what we thought . . ."

Colonel Blount looked at him gravely for some time. Then he said, "I think that an admirable idea. I don't see any reason at all why I shouldn't. How much do you want?"

"That's really terribly good of you, sir. . . . Well, you know, just enough to live on quietly for a bit. I hardly know . . ."

"Well, would a thousand pounds be any help?"

"Yes, it would indeed. We shall both be terribly grateful."

"Not at all, my dear boy. Not at all. What did you say your name was?"

"Adam Symes."

Colonel Blount went to the table and wrote out a cheque. "There you are," he said. "Now don't go giving that away to another drunk major."

98

"Really, sir! I don't know how to thank you. Nina . . ."

"Not another word. Now I expect that you will want to be off to London again. We'll send Mrs. Florin across to the Rectory and make the Rector drive you to the station. Useful having a neighbour with a motor car. They charge fivepence on the buses from here to Aylesbury. *Robbers.*"

It does not befall many young men to be given a thousand pounds by a complete stranger twice on successive evenings. Adam laughed aloud in the Rector's car as they drove to the station. The Rector, who had been in the middle of writing a sermon and resented with daily increasing feeling Colonel Blount's neighbourly appropriation of his car and himself, kept his eyes fixed on the streaming windscreen pretending not to notice. Adam laughed all the way to Aylesbury, sitting and holding his knees and shaking all over. The Rector could hardly bring himself to say good night when they parted in the station yard.

There was half an hour to wait for a train and the leaking roof and wet railway lines had a sobering effect on Adam. He bought an evening paper, On the front page was an exquisitely funny photograph of

Miss Runcible in Hawaiian costume tumbling down the steps of No. 10, Downing Street. The Government had fallen that afternoon, he read, being defeated on a motion rising from the answer to a question about the treatment of Miss Runcible by Customs House officers. It was generally held in Parliamentary circles that the deciding factor in this reverse had been the revolt of the Liberals and the Nonconformist members at the revelations of the life that was led at No. 10, Downing Street during Sir James Brown's tenancy. The *Evening Standard* had a leading article, which drew a fine analogy between Public and Domestic Purity, between sobriety in the family and in the State.

There was another small paragraph which interested Adam.

"Tragedy in West-End Hotel.

"The death occurred early this morning at a private hotel in Dover Street of Miss Florence Ducane, described as being of independent means, following an accident in which Miss Ducane fell from a chandelier which she was attempting to mend. The inquest will be held tomorrow, which will be followed by the

100

*cremation at Golders Green. Miss Ducane, who was
formerly connected with the stage, was well known in
business circles."*

Which only showed, thought Adam, how much
better Lottie Crump knew the business of avoiding
undesirable publicity than Sir James Brown.

When Adam reached London the rain had stopped,
but there was a thin fog drifting in belts before a
damp wind. The station was crowded with office
workers hurrying with attaché cases and evening papers to catch their evening trains home, coughing and
sneezing as they went. They still wore their poppies.
Adam went to a telephone-box and rang up Nina. She
had left a message for him that she was having cocktails at Margot Metroland's house. He drove to
Shepheard's.

"Lottie," he said, "I've got a thousand pounds."

"Have you, now," said Lottie indifferently. She
lived on the assumption that everyone she knew always had several thousand pounds. It was to her as
though he had said, "Lottie, I have a tall hat."

"Can you lend me some money till tomorrow till I
cash the cheque?"

101

"What a boy you are for borrowing. Just like your poor father. Here, you in the corner, lend Mr. What-d'you-call-him some money."

A tall Guardsman shook his retreating forehead and twirled his moustaches.

"No good coming to me, Lottie," he said in a voice trained to command.

"Mean hound," said Lottie. "Where's that American?"

Judge Skimp, who, since his experiences that morning, had become profoundly Anglophile, produced two ten-pound notes. "I shall be only too proud and honoured . . ." he said.

"Good old Judge Thingummy," said Lottie. "That's the way."

Adam hurried out into the hall as another bottle of champagne popped festively in the parlour.

"Doge, ring up the Daimler Hire Company and order a car in my name. Tell it to go round to Lady Metroland's—Pastmaster House, Hill Street," he said. Then he put on his hat and walked down Hay Hill, swinging an umbrella and laughing again, only more quietly, to himself.

At Lady Metroland's he kept on his coat and waited in the hall.

102

"Will you please tell Miss Blount I've called for her? No, I won't go up."

He looked at the hats on the table. Clearly there was quite a party. Two or three silk hats of people who had dressed early, the rest soft and black like his own. Then he began to dance again, jigging to himself in simple high spirits.

In a minute Nina came down the broad Adam staircase.

"Darling, why didn't you come up? It's so rude. Margot is longing to see you."

"I'm so sorry, Nina. I couldn't face a party. I'm so excited."

"Why, what's happened?"

"Everything. I'll tell you in the car."

"Car?"

"Yes, it'll be here in a minute. We're going down to the country for dinner. I can't tell you how clever I've been."

"But what have you done, darling? Do stop dancing about."

"Can't stop. You've no idea how clever I am."

"Adam. Are you tight again?"

"Look out of the window and see if you can see a Daimler waiting."

"Adam, what *have* you been doing? I will be told."

"Look," said Adam, producing the cheque. "Whatcher think of that?" he added in Cockney.

"*My dear,* a thousand pounds. Did papa give you that?"

"I earned it," said Adam. "Oh, I earned it. You should have seen the luncheon I ate and the jokes I read. I'm going to be married tomorrow. Oh, Nina, would Margot hate it if I sang in her hall?"

"She'd simply loathe it, darling, and so should I. I'm going to take care of that cheque. You remember what happened the last time you were given a thousand pounds."

"That's what your papa said."

"Did you tell him that?"

"I told him everything—and he gave me a thousand pounds."

". . . Poor Adam . . ." said Nina suddenly.

"Why did you say that?"

"I don't know. . . . I believe this is your car. . . ."

"Nina, why did you say 'Poor Adam'?"

". . . Did I? . . . Oh, I don't know. . . . Oh, I do adore you so."

"I'm going to be married tomorrow. Are you?"

104

"Yes, I expect so, dear."

The chauffeur got rather bored while they tried to decide where they would dine. At every place he suggested they gave a little wail of dismay. "But that's sure to be full of awful people, we know," they said. Maidenhead, Thame, Brighton, he suggested. Finally they decided to go to Arundel.

"It'll be nearly nine before we get there," the chauffeur said. "Now there's a very nice hotel at Bray. . . ."

But they went to Arundel.

"We'll be married tomorrow," said Adam in the car. "And we won't ask anybody to the wedding at all. And we'll go abroad at once, and just not come back till I've written all those books. Nina, isn't it divine? Where shall we go?"

"Anywhere you like, only rather warm, don't you think?"

"I don't believe you really think we are going to be married, Nina, do you, or do you?"

"I don't know . . . it's only that I don't believe that really divine things like that ever do happen. . . . I don't know why. . . . Oh, I do like you so much tonight. If only you *knew* how sweet you looked skipping about in Margot's hall all by yourself. I'd been watching you for hours before I came down."

"I shall send the car back," said Adam, as they drove through Pulborough. "We can go home by train."

"If there is a train."

"There's bound to be," said Adam. But this raised a question in both their minds that had been unobtrusively agitating them throughout the journey. Neither said any more on the subject, but there was a distinct air of constraint in the Daimler from Pulborough onwards.

This question was settled when they reached the hotel at Arundel.

"We want dinner," said Adam, "and a room for the night."

"*Darling,* am I going to be seduced?"

"I'm afraid you are. Do you mind terribly?"

"Not as much as all that," said Nina, and added in Cockney, "Charmed, I'm sure."

Everyone else had finished dinner. They dined alone in a corner of the coffee-room, while the other waiter laid the tables for breakfast, looking at them resentfully. It was the dreariest kind of English dinner. After dinner the lounge was awful; there were some golfers in dinner-jackets playing bridge, and

106

two old ladies. Adam and Nina went across the stable-yard to the tap-room and sat until closing time in a warm haze of tobacco smoke listening to the intermittent gossip of the townspeople. They sat hand-in-hand, unembarrassed; after the first minute no one noticed them. Just before closing time Adam stood a round of drinks. They said:

"Good health, sir. Best respects, madam," and the barman said, "Come along, please. Finish your drinks, please," in a peculiar sing-song tone.

There was a clock chiming as they crossed the yard and a slightly drunk farmer trying to start up his car. Then they went up an oak staircase lined with blunderbusses and coaching prints to their room.

They had no night things (the chambermaid remarked on this next day to the young man who worked at the wireless shop, saying that that was the worst of being in a main-road hotel. You got all sorts).

Adam undressed very quickly and got into bed; Nina more slowly arranging her clothes on the chair and fingering the ornaments on the chimney-piece with less than her usual self-possession.

At last she put out the light.

"Do you know," she said, trembling slightly as she

got into bed, "this is the first time this has happened to me?"

"It's great fun," said Adam, "I promise you."

"I'm sure it is," said Nina seriously, "I wasn't saying anything against it. It was only saying that it hadn't happened before. . . . Oh, Adam. . . ."

"And you said that really divine things didn't happen," said Adam in the middle of the night.

"I don't think that this is at all divine," said Nina. "It's given me a pain. And—my dear, that reminds me. I've something terribly important to say to you in the morning."

"What?"

"Not now, darling. Let's go to sleep for a little, don't you think?"

Before Nina was properly awake Adam dressed and went out into the rain to get a shave. He came back bringing two toothbrushes and a bright red celluloid comb. Nina sat up in bed and combed her hair. She put Adam's coat over her back.

"My dear, you look exactly like *La Vie Parisienne*," said Adam, turning round from brushing his teeth.

Then she threw off the coat and jumped out of bed, and he told her that she looked like a fashion drawing from *Vogue,* only without any clothes on. Nina was rather pleased about that, but she said that it was cold and that she still had a pain, only not so bad as it was. Then she dressed and they went downstairs.

Everyone else had had breakfast and the waiters were laying the tables for luncheon.

"By the way," said Adam. "You said there was something you wanted to say."

"Oh, yes, so there is. My dear, something quite awful."

"Do tell me."

"Well, it's about that cheque papa gave you. I'm afraid it won't help us as much as you thought."

"But, darling, it's a thousand pounds, isn't it?"

"Just look at it, my sweet." She took it out of her bag and handed it across the table.

"I don't see anything wrong with it," said Adam.

"Not the signature?"

"Why, good lord, the old idiot's signed it 'Charlie Chaplin.' "

"That's what I mean, darling."

"But can't we get him to alter it? He must be dotty. I'll go down and see him again today."

"I shouldn't do that, dear . . . don't you see. . . . Of course, he's very old, and . . . I dare say you may have made things sound a little odd . . . don't you think, dear, *he* must have thought *you* a little dotty? . . . I mean . . . perhaps . . . that cheque was a kind of joke."

"Well, I'm damned . . . this really is a bore. When everything seemed to be going so well, too. When did you notice the signature, Nina?"

"As soon as you showed it to me, at Margot's. Only you looked so happy I didn't like to say anything. . . . You did look happy, you know, Adam, and so sweet. I think I really fell in love with you for the first time when I saw you dancing all alone in the hall."

"Well, I'm damned," said Adam again. "The old devil."

"Anyway, you've had some fun out of it, haven't you . . . or haven't you?"

"Haven't *you?*"

"My dear, I never hated anything so much in my life . . . still, as long as you enjoyed it that's something."

"I say, Nina," said Adam after some time, "we shan't be able to get married after all."

"No, I'm afraid not."

"It *is* a bore, isn't it?"

Later he said, "I expect that parson thought I was dotty too."

And later, "As a matter of fact, it's rather a good joke, don't you think?"

"I think it's divine."

In the train Nina said: "It's awful to think that I shall probably never, as long as I live, see you dancing like that again all by yourself."

VI

HAT evening Lady Metroland gave a party for Mrs. Melrose Ape. Adam found the telegram of invitation waiting for him on his return to Shepheard's. (Lottie had already used the prepaid reply to do some betting with. Someone had given her a tip for the November Handicap and she wanted to "make her little flutter" before she forgot the name.) He also found an invitation to luncheon from Simon Balcairn.

The food at Shepheard's tends to be mostly game-pie—quite black inside and full of beaks and shot and inexplicable vertebræ—so Adam was quite pleased to lunch with Simon Balcairn, though he knew there must be some slightly sinister motive behind this sudden hospitality.

They lunched *Chez Espinosa*, the second most expensive restaurant in London; it was full of oilcloth
112

and Lalique glass, and the sort of people who liked that sort of think went there continually and said how awful it was.

"I hope you don't mind coming to this awful restaurant," said Balcairn. "The truth is that I get meals free if I mention them occasionally in my page. Not drinks, unfortunately. Who's here, Alphonse?" he asked the *maître d'hôtel*.

Alphonse handed him the typewritten slip that was always kept for gossip writers.

"H'm, yes. Quite a good list this morning, Alphonse. I'll do what I can about it."

"Thank you, sir. A table for two? A cocktail?"

"No, I don't think I want a cocktail. I really haven't time. Will you have one, Adam? They aren't very good here."

"No, thanks," said Adam.

"Sure?" said Balcairn, already making for their table.

When they were being helped to caviare he looked at the wine list.

"The lager is rather good," he said. "What would you like to drink?"

"Whatever you're having. . . . I think some lager would be lovely."

113

"Two small bottles of lager, please. . . . Are you sure you really like that better than anything?"

"Yes, really, thank you."

Simon Balcairn looked about him gloomily, occasionally adding a new name to his list. (It is so depressing to be in a profession in which literally all conversation is "shop.")

Presently he said, with a deadly air of carelessness:

"Margot Metroland's got a party tonight, hasn't she? Are you going?"

"I think, probably. I usually like Margot's parties, don't you?"

"Yes. . . . Adam, I'll tell you a very odd thing. She hasn't sent me an invitation to this one."

"I expect she will. I only got mine this morning."

". . . Yes . . . who's that woman just come in in the fur coat? I know her so well by sight."

"Isn't it Lady Everyman?"

"Yes, of course." Another name was added to the list. Balcairn paused in utmost gloom and ate some salad. "The thing is . . . she told Agatha Runcible she wasn't *going* to ask me."

"Why not?"

"Apparently she's in a rage about something I said about something she said about Miles."

114

"People do take things so seriously," said Adam encouragingly.

"It means ruin for me," said Lord Balcairn. "Isn't that Pamela Popham?"

"I haven't the least idea."

"I'm sure it is . . . I must look up the spelling in the stud book when I get back. I got into awful trouble about spelling the other day. . . . Ruin. . . . She's asked Vanburgh."

"Well, he's some sort of cousin, isn't he?"

"It's so damned unfair. All my cousins are in lunatic asylums or else they live in the country and do indelicate things with wild animals . . . except my mamma, and that's worse. . . . They were furious at the office about Van getting that Downing Street 'scoop.' If I miss this party I may as well leave Fleet Street for good . . . I may as well put my head into a gas-oven and have done with it . . . I'm sure if Margot knew how much it meant to me she wouldn't mind my coming."

Great tears stood in his eyes threatening to overflow.

"All this last week," he said, "I've been reduced to making up my page from the Court Circular and Debrett. . . . No one ever asks me anywhere now. . . ."

115

"I'll tell you what," said Adam, "I know Margot pretty well. If you like I'll ring her up and ask if I may bring you."

"Will you? Will you, Adam? If only you really would. Let's go and do it at once. We've no time for coffee or liqueurs. Quick, we can telephone from my office . . . yes, that black hat and my umbrella, no, I've lost the number . . . there, no, there, oh do hurry. . . . Yes, a taxi. . . ."

They were out in the street and into a taxi before Adam had time to say any more. Soon they were imbedded in a traffic block in the Strand, and after a time they reached Balcairn's office in Fleet Street.

They went up to a tiny room with "Social" written on the glass of the door. Its interior seemed not to justify its name. There was one chair, a typewriter, a telephone, some books of reference and a considerable litter of photographs. Balcairn's immediate superior sat in the one chair.

"Hullo," she said. "So you're back. Where you been?"

"Espinosa. Here's the list."

The social editress read it through. "Can't have Kitty Blackwater," she said. "Had her yesterday. Others'll do. Write 'em down to a couple of paragraphs. Suppose you didn't notice what they were wearing?"

"Yes," said Balcairn eagerly. "All of them."

"Well, you won't have room to use it. We got to keep everything down for Lady M.'s party. I've cut out the D. of Devonshire altogether. By the way, the photograph you used yesterday wasn't the present Countess of Everyman. It's an old one of the Dowager. We had 'em both on the 'phone about it, going on something awful. That's *you* again. Got your invite for tonight?"

"Not yet."

"You better get it quick. I got to have a first-hand story before we go to press, see? By the way, know anything about this? Lady R.'s maid sent it in today." She picked up a slip of paper: " 'Rumoured engagement broken off between Adam Fenwick-Symes, only son of the late Professor Oliver Fenwick-Symes, and Nina Blount, of Doubting Hall, Aylesbury.' Never heard of either. Ain't even been announced, so far as I'm aware of."

"You'd better ask him. This is Adam Symes."

"Hullo, no offence meant, I'm sure. . . . What about it?"

"It is neither announced or broken off."

"N.B.G. in fact, eh? Then *that* goes *there*." She put the slip into the wastepaper basket. "That girl's sent us a lot of bad stuff lately. Well, I'm off for a bit of lunch. I'll be over at the Garden Club if anything urgent turns up. So long."

The editress went out, banging the door labelled "Social," and whistled as she went down the passage.

"You see how they treat me," said Lord Balcairn. "They were all over me when I first arrived. I do so wish I were dead."

"Don't cry," said Adam, "it's too shy-making."

"I can't help it . . . oh, do come in."

The door marked "Social" opened and a small boy came in.

"Lord Circumference's butler downstairs with some engagements and a divorce."

"Tell him to leave them."

"Very good, my lord."

"That's the only person in this office who's ever polite to me," said Balcairn as the messenger disappeared. "I wish I had something to leave him in my will. . . . Do ring up Margot. Then I shall at any rate know the worst. . . . Come in."

"Gentleman of the name of General Strapper downstairs. Wants to see you very particular."

118

"What about?"

"Couldn't say, my lord, but he's got a whip. Seems very put out about something."

"Tell him the social editor is having luncheon. . . . Do ring up Margot."

Adam said, "Margot, may I bring someone with me tonight?"

"Well, Adam, I really don't think you can. I can't imagine how everyone's going to get in as it is. I'm terribly sorry, who is it?"

"Simon Balcairn. He's particularly anxious to come."

"I dare say he is. I'm rather against that young man. He's written things about me in the papers."

"Please, Margot."

"Certainly not. I won't have him inside my house. I've only asked Van on the strictest understanding that he doesn't write anything about it. I don't wish to have anything more to do with Simon Balcairn."

"My dear, how *rich* you sound."

"I feel my full income when that young man is mentioned. Good-bye. See you tonight."

"You needn't tell me," said Balcairn. "I know what she's said . . . it's no good, is it?"

"I'm afraid not."

119

"Done for . . ." said Balcairn. ". . . End of the tether. . . ." He turned over some slips of paper listlessly. "Would it interest you to hear that Agatha and Archie are engaged?"

"I don't believe it."

"Neither do I. One of our people has just sent it in. Half of what they send us is lies, and the other half libel . . . they sent us a long story about Miles and Pamela Popham having spent last night at Arundel. . . . But we couldn't use it even if it were true, which it obviously isn't, knowing Miles. Thank you for doing what you could . . . good-bye."

Downstairs in the outer office there was an altercation in progress. A large man of military appearance was shaking and stamping in front of a middle-aged woman. Adam recognized the social editress.

"Answer me, yes or no," the big man was saying. "Are you or are you not responsible for this damnable lie about my daughter?"

(He had read in Simon Balcairn's column that his daughter had been seen at a night club. To anyone better acquainted with Miss Strapper's habits of life the paragraph was particularly reticent.)

"Yes or no," cried the General, "or I'll shake the life out of you."

120

"No."

"Then who is? Let me get hold of the cad who wrote it. Where is he?" roared the General.

"Upstairs," the social editress managed to say.

"More trouble for Simon," thought Adam.

Adam went to pick Nina up at her flat. They had arranged to go to a cinema together. She said, "You're much later than you said. It's so boring to be late for a talkie."

He said, "Talkies are boring, anyhow."

They treated each other quite differently after their night's experiences. Adam was inclined to be egotistical and despondent; Nina was rather grown-up and disillusioned and distinctly cross. Adam began to say that as far as he could see he would have to live on at Shepheard's now for the rest of his life, or at any rate for the rest of Lottie's life, as it wouldn't be fair to leave without paying the bill.

Then Nina said, "Do be amusing, Adam. I can't bear you when you're not amusing."

Then Adam began to tell her about Simon Balcairn and Margot's party. He described how he had seen Simon being horse-whipped in the middle of the office.

121

Nina said, "Yes, that's amusing. Go on like that."

The story of Simon's whipping lasted them all the way to the cinema. They were very late for the film Nina wanted to see, and that set them back again. They didn't speak for a long time. Then Nina said *à propos* of the film, "All this fuss about sleeping together. For physical pleasure I'd sooner go to my dentist any day."

Adam said, "You'll enjoy it more next time."

Nina said, *"Next time,"* and told him that he took too much for granted.

Adam said that that was a phrase which only prostitutes used.

Then they started a real quarrel which lasted all through the film and all the way to Nina's flat and all the time she was cutting up a lemon and making a cocktail, until Adam said that if she didn't stop going on he would ravish her there and then on her own hearth-rug.

Then Nina went on, provocatively.

But by the time that Adam went to dress she had climbed down enough to admit that perhaps love was a thing one could grow to be fond of after a time, like smoking a pipe. Still she maintained that it made

122

one feel very ill at first, and she doubted if it was worth it.

Then they began to argue at the top of the lift about whether acquired tastes were ever worth acquiring. Adam said it was imitation, and that it was natural to man to be imitative, so that acquired tastes were natural. But the presence of the lift boy stopped that argument coming to a solution as the other had done.

The truth is that like so many people of their age and class, Adam and Nina were suffering from being sophisticated about sex before they were at all widely experienced.

"My, ain't this classy," said Divine Discontent.

"It's all right," said Chastity in a worldly voice. "Nothing to make a song and dance about."

"Who's making a song and dance? I just said it was classy—and it *is* classy, ain't it?"

"I suppose everything's classy to *some* people."

"Now you two," said Temperance, who had been put in charge of the angels for the evening, "don't you start anything in here, not with your wings on. Mrs. Ape won't stand for scrapping in wings, and you know it."

123

"Who's starting anything?"

"Well, you are then."

"Oh, it's no use talking to Chastity. She's too high and mighty to be an angel now. Went out for a drive with Mrs. Panrast in a Rolls Royce," said Fortitude. "I saw her. I was *so* sorry it rained all the time, or it might have been quite enjoyable, mightn't it, Chastity?"

"Well, you ought to be glad. Leaves the *men* for you, Fortitude. Only they don't seem to want to take advantage, do they?"

Then they talked about men for some time. Divine Discontent thought the second footman had nice eyes.

"And he knows it," said Temperance.

They were all having supper together in what was still called the schoolroom in Lady Metroland's house. From the window they could see the guests arriving for the party. In spite of the rain quite a large crowd had collected on either side of the awning to criticize the cloaks with appreciative "oohs" and "ahs" or contemptuous sniffs. Cars and taxis drove up in close succession. Lady Circumference splashed up the street in goloshes, wearing a high fender of diamonds under a tartan umbrella. The Bright Young

124

People came popping all together, out of someone's electric brougham like a litter of pigs, and ran squealing up the steps. Some "gate-crashers" who had made the mistake of coming in Victorian fancy dress were detected and repulsed. They hurried home to change for a second assault. No one wanted to miss Mrs. Ape's début.

But the angels were rather uneasy. They had been dressed ever since seven o'clock in their white shifts, gold sashes and wings. It was now past ten, and the strain was beginning to tell, for it was impossible to sit back comfortably in wings.

"Oh, I wish they'd hurry up so we could get it over," said Creative Endeavour. "Mrs. Ape said we could have some champagne afterwards if we sang nice."

"I don't mind betting *she's* doing herself pretty well, down there."

"*Chastity!*"

"Oh, *all* right."

Then the footman with the nice eyes came to clear the table. He gave them a friendly wink as he shut the door. "Pretty creatures," he thought. "Blooming shame that they're so religious . . . wasting the best years of their lives."

125

There had been a grave debate in the servants' hall about the exact status of angels. Even Mr. Blenkinsop, the butler, had been uncertain. "Angels are certainly not guests," he had said, "and I don't think they are deputations. Nor they ain't governesses either, nor clergy not strictly speaking; they're not entertainers, because entertainers *dine* nowadays, the more's the pity."

"I believe they're decorators," said Mrs. Blouse, "or else charitable workers."

"Charitable workers are governesses, Mrs. Blouse. There is nothing to be gained by multiplying social distinctions indefinitely. Decorators are either guests or workmen."

After further discussion the conclusion was reached that angels were nurses, and that became the official ruling of the household. But the second footman was of the opinion that they were just "young persons," pure and simple, "and very nice too," for nurses cannot, except in very rare cases, be winked at, and clearly angels could.

"What we want to know, Chastity," said Creative Endeavour, "is how you come to take up with Mrs. Panrast at all."

"Yes," said the angels, "yes. It's not like *you*,

Chastity, to go riding in a motor car with a woman."
They fluttered their feathers in a menacing way.
"Let's third-degree her," said Humility with rather
nasty relish.

(There was a system of impromptu jurisdiction
among the angels which began with innuendo, went
on to cross-examination, pinches and slaps and ended,
as a rule, in tears and kisses.)

Faced by this circle of spiteful and haloed faces,
Chastity began to lose her air of superiority.

"Why shouldn't I ride with a friend," she asked
plaintively, "without all you girls pitching on me like
this?"

"*Friend*," said Creative Endeavour. "You never
saw her before today," and she gave her a nasty pinch
just above the elbow.

"*Ooooh!*" said Chastity. "*OOh, please* . . . beast."

Then they all pinched her all over, but precisely
and judiciously, so as not to disturb her wings or
halo, for this was no orgy (sometimes in their bedrooms, they gave way, but not here, in Lady Metroland's schoolroom, before an important first night).

"Ooh," said Chastity. "*OOh, ow, ooh, ow. Please*,
beasts, swine, cads . . . *please* . . . ooh . . . well,
if you must know, I thought she *was* a man."

"Thought she was a *man*, Chastity? That doesn't sound right to me."

"Well, she looks like a man and—and she *goes on* like a man. I saw her sitting at a table in a tea-shop. She hadn't got a hat on, and I couldn't see her skirt . . . ooh . . . how can I tell you if you keep pinching . . . and she smiled and so, well, I went and had some tea with her, and she said would I go out with her in her motor car, and I said yes and, ooh, I wish I hadn't now."

"What did she say in the motor car, Chastity?"

"I forget—nothing much."

"Oh, what." "Do tell us." "We'll never pinch you again if you tell us." "I'm sorry if I hurt you, Chastity, do *tell* me." "You'd *better* tell us."

"No, I can't, *really*—I don't remember, I tell you."

"Give her another little nip, girls."

"Ooh, ooh, ooh, *stop*. I'll tell you."

Their heads were close together and they were so deeply engrossed in the story that they did not hear Mrs. Ape's entry.

"Back-chat again," said a terrible voice. "Girls, I'm sick ashamed of you."

Mrs. Ape looked magnificent in a gown of heavy gold brocade embroidered with texts.

"I'm sick ashamed of you," repeated Mrs. Ape, "and you've made Chastity cry again, just before the big act. If you must bully someone, *why* choose Chastity? You all know by this time that crying always gives her a red nose. How do *I* look, I should like to know, standing up in front of a lot of angels with red noses. You don't ever think of nothing but your own pleasures, do you? *Sluts.*" This last word was spoken with a depth of expression that set the angels trembling. "There'll be no champagne for anyone tonight, see. And if you don't sing perfectly, I'll give the whole lot of you a good hiding, see. Now, come on, now, and for the love of the Lamb, Chastity, *do something to your nose.* They'll think it's a temperance meeting to see you like that."

It was a brilliant scene into which the disconsolate angels trooped two minutes later. Margot Metroland shook hands with each of them as they came to the foot of the staircase, appraising them, one by one, with an expert eye.

"You don't look happy, my dear," she found time to say to Chastity, as she led them across the ball-

129

room to their platform, banked in orchids at the far end. "If you feel you want a change, let me know later, and I can get you a job in South America. *I mean it.*"

"Oh, thank you," said Chastity, "but I could never leave Mrs. Ape."

"Well, think it over, child. You're far too pretty a girl to waste your time singing hymns. Tell that other girl, the red-headed one, that I can probably find a place for her, too."

"What, Humility? Don't you have nothing to do with her. She's a fiend."

"Well, some men like rough stuff, but I don't want anyone who makes trouble with the other girls."

"She makes trouble all right. Look at that bruise."

"My dear!"

Margot Metroland and Mrs. Ape led the angels up the steps between the orchids and stood them at the back of the platform facing the room. Chastity stood next to Creative Endeavour.

"Please, Chastity, I'm sorry if we hurt you," said Creative Endeavour. "*I* didn't pinch hard, did I?"

"Yes," said Chastity. "Like hell you did."

A slightly sticky hand tried to take hers, but she

130

clenched her fist. She would go to South America and work for Lady Metroland . . . and she wouldn't say anything about it to Humility either. She stared straight in front of her, saw Mrs. Panrast and dropped her eyes.

The ballroom was filled with little gilt chairs and the chairs with people. Lord Vanburgh, conveniently seated near the door, through which he could slip away to the telephone, was taking them all in. They were almost all, in some way or another, notable. The motives for Margot Metroland's second marriage * had been mixed, but entirely worldly; chief among them had been the desire to re-establish her somewhat shaken social position, and her party that night testified to her success, for while many people can entertain the Prime Minister and the Duchess of Stayle and Lady Circumference, and anybody can, and often against her will does, entertain Miles Malpractice and Agatha Runcible, it is only a very confident hostess who will invite both these sets together at the same time, differing, as they do, upon almost all questions of principle and deportment. Standing near Vanburgh, by the door, was a figure who seemed

* See *Decline and Fall*.

131

in himself to typify the change that had come over Pastmaster House when Margot Beste-Chetwynd became Lady Metroland; an unobtrusive man of rather less than average height, whose black beard, falling in tight burnished curls, nearly concealed the order of St. Michael and St. George which he wore round his neck; he wore a large signet ring on the little finger of his left hand outside his white glove; there was an orchid in his buttonhole. His eyes, youthful but grave, wandered among the crowd; occasionally he bowed with grace and decision. Several people were asking about him.

"See the beaver with the medal," said Humility to Faith.

"Who is that *very* important young man?" asked Mrs. Blackwater of Lady Throbbing.

"I don't know, dear. He bowed to *you.*"

"He bowed to *you,* dear."

"How very nice . . . I wasn't quite sure. . . . He reminds me a little of dear Prince Anrep."

"It's so nice in these days, isn't it, dearest, to see someone who really looks . . . don't you think?"

"You mean the beard?"

"The beard among other things, darling."

132

Father Rothschild was conspiring with Mr. Outrage and Lord Metroland. He stopped short in the middle of his sentence.

"Forgive me," he said, "but there are spies everywhere. That man with the beard, do you know him?"

Lord Metroland thought vaguely he had something to do with the Foreign Office; Mr. Outrage seemed to remember having seen him before.

"Exactly," said Father Rothschild, "I think it would be better if we continued our conversation in private. I have been watching him. *He is bowing across the room to empty places and to people whose backs are turned to him."* The Great Men withdrew to Lord Metroland's study. Father Rothschild closed the door silently and looked behind the curtains.

"Shall I lock the door?" asked Lord Metroland.

"No," said the Jesuit. "A lock does not prevent a spy from hearing; but it does hinder us, inside, from catching the spy."

"Well, I should never have thought of that," said Mr. Outrage in frank admiration.

"How pretty Nina Blount is," said Lady Throbbing, busy from the front row with her lorgnette.

"but don't you think, a little changed; almost as though . . ."

"You notice everything, darling."

"When you get to our age, dear, there is so little left, but I do believe Miss Blount must have had an experience . . . she's sitting next to Miles. You know I heard from Edward tonight. He's on his way back. It will be a great blow for Miles because he's been living in Edward's house all this time. To tell you the truth I'm a little glad because from what I hear from Anne Opalthorpe, who lives opposite, the things that go on . . . he's got a friend staying there now. Such an odd man—a dirt-track racer. But then it's no use attempting to disguise the fact, *is* there? . . . There's Mrs. Panrast . . . yes, dear, of course you know her, she used to be Eleanor Balcairn . . . now *why* does dear Margot ask anyone like that, do you think? . . . It is not as though Margot was so innocent . . . and there's Lord Monomark . . . yes, the man who owns those *amusing* papers . . . they say that he and Margot, but *before* her marriage, of course (her second marriage, I mean), but you never know, do you, how things *crop* up again? . . . I wonder where Peter Pastmaster is? . . . He never stays to Margot's parties . . . he was at dinner, of course, and, my dear, *how* he drank. . . . He can't be more than twenty-one. . . . Oh, so that is Mrs. Ape. What a coarse face . . . no dear, of course she can't hear . . . she looks like a *procureuse* . . . but perhaps I shouldn't say that *here*, should I?"

Adam came and sat next to Nina.

"Hullo," they said to each other.

"My dear, do look at Mary Mouse's new young man," said Nina.

Adam looked and saw that Mary was sitting next to the Maharajah of Pukkapore.

"I call that a pretty pair," he said.

"Oh, how bored I feel," said Nina.

Mr. Benfleet was there talking to two poets. They said, ". . . And I wrote to tell William that I didn't write the review, but it was true that Tony did read me the review over the telephone when I was very sleepy before he sent it in. I thought it was best to tell him the truth because he would hear it from Tony, anyway. Only I said I advised him not to publish it just as I had advised William not to publish the book in the first place. Well, Tony rang up Michael and told him that I'd said that William thought Michael had

135

written the review because of the reviews I had written of Michael's book last November, though, as a matter of fact, it was Tony himself who wrote it. . . ."

"Too bad," said Mr. Benfleet. "Too bad."

". . . But is that any reason, even if I had written it, why Michael should tell Tony that I had stolen five pounds from William?"

"Certainly not," said Mr. Benfleet. "Too bad."

"Of course, they're *simply* not *gentlemen,* either of them. That's all it is, only one's shy of saying it nowadays."

Mr. Benfleet shook his head sadly and sympathetically.

Then Mrs. Melrose Ape stood up to speak. A hush fell in the ballroom beginning at the back and spreading among the gilt chairs until only Mrs. Blackwater's voice was heard exquisitely articulating some details of Lady Metroland's past. Then she, too, was silent and Mrs. Ape began her oration about Hope.

"Brothers and Sisters," she said in a hoarse, stirring voice. Then she paused and allowed her eyes, renowned throughout three continents for their magnetism, to travel among the gilded chairs. (It was one

136

of her favourite openings.) *"Just you look at your-selves,"* she said.

Magically, self-doubt began to spread in the audience. Mrs. Panrast stirred uncomfortably; had that silly little girl been talking, she wondered.

"Darling," whispered Miss Runcible, "is my nose awful?"

Nina thought how once, only twenty-four hours ago, she had been in love. Mr. Benfleet thought should he have made it three per cent. on the tenth thousand. The gate-crashers wondered whether it would not have been better to have stayed at home. (Once in Kansas City Mrs. Ape had got no further than these opening words; there had been a tornado of emotion and all the seats in the hall had been broken to splinters. It was there that Humility had joined the angels.) There were a thousand things in Lady Throbbing's past. . . . Every heart found something to bemoan.

"She's got 'em again," whispered Creative Endeavour. "Got 'em stiff."

Lord Vanburgh slipped from the room to telephone through some racy paragraphs about fashionable piety.

Mary Mouse shed two little tears and felt for the brown, bejewelled hand of the Maharajah.

137

But suddenly on that silence vibrant with self-accusation broke the organ voice of England, the hunting-cry of the *ancien régime*. Lady Circumference gave a resounding snort of disapproval:

"What a damned impudent woman," she said.

Adam and Nina and Miss Runcible began to giggle, and Margot Metroland for the first time in her many parties was glad to realize that the guest of the evening was going to be a failure. It had been an awkward moment.

In the study Father Rothschild and Mr. Outrage were plotting with enthusiasm. Lord Metroland was smoking a cigar and wondering how soon he could get away. He wanted to hear Mrs. Ape and to have another look at those angels. There was one with red hair. . . . Besides all this statesmanship and foreign policy had always bored him. In his years in the Commons he had always liked a good scrap, and often thought a little wistfully of those orgies of competitive dissimulation in which he had risen to eminence. Even now, when some straightforward, easily intelligible subject was under discussion, such as poor people's wages or public art, he enjoyed every now and then making a sonorous speech to the Upper House.

138

But this sort of thing was not at all in his line
Suddenly Father Rothschild turned out the light.

"There's someone coming down the passage," he said. "Quick, get behind the curtains."

"Really, Rothschild . . ." said Mr. Outrage.

"I say . . ." said Lord Metroland.

"Quick," said Father Rothschild.

The three statesmen hid themselves. Lord Metroland, still smoking, his head thrown back and his cigar erect. They heard the door open. The light was turned on. A match was struck. Then came the slight tinkle of the telephone as someone lifted the receiver.

"Central ten thousand," said a slightly muffled voice.

"Now," said Father Rothschild, and stepped through the curtain.

The bearded stranger who had excited his suspicions was standing at the table smoking one of Lord Metroland's cigars and holding the telephone.

"Oh, hullo," he said, "I didn't know you were here. Just thought I'd use the telephone. So sorry. Won't disturb you. Jolly party, isn't it? Good-bye."

"Stay exactly where you are," said Father Rothschild, "and take off that beard."

"Damned if I do," said the stranger crossly. "It's

139

no use talking to me as though I were one of your choir boys . . . you old *bully*."

"Take off that beard," said Father Rothschild.

"Take off that beard," said Lord Metroland and the Prime Minister, emerging suddenly from behind the curtain.

This concurrence of Church and State, coming so unexpectedly after an evening of prolonged embarrassment, was too much for Simon.

"Oh, all right," he said, "if you *will* make such a *thing* about it . . . it hurts too frightfully, if you knew . . . it ought to be soaked in hot water . . . ooh . . . ow."

He gave some tugs at the black curls, and bit by bit they came away.

"*There*," he said. "Now I should go and make Lady Throbbing take off her wig. . . . I should have a really jolly evening while you're about it, if I were you."

"I seem to have over-estimated the gravity of the situation," said Father Rothschild.

"Who is it, after all this?" said Mr. Outrage. "Where are those detectives? What does it all mean?"

140

"That," said Father Rothschild bitterly, "is *Mr. Chatterbox.*"

"Never heard of him. I don't believe there is such a person. . . . *Chatterbox,* indeed . . . you make us hide behind a curtain and then you tell us that some young man in a false beard is called Chatterbox. Really, Rothschild . . ."

"Lord Balcairn," said Lord Metroland, "will you kindly leave my house immediately?"

"*Is* this young man called Chatterbox or is he not? . . . Upon my soul, I believe you're all crazy."

"Oh, yes, I'm going," said Simon. "You didn't think I was going to go back to the party like this, *did* you? —or did you?" Indeed, he looked very odd with little patches of black hair still adhering to parts of his chin and cheeks.

"Lord Monomark is here this evening, I shall certainly inform him of your behaviour. . . ."

"He writes for the papers," Father Rothschild tried to explain to the Prime Minister.

"Well, damn it, so do I, but I don't wear a false beard and call myself Chatterbox. . . . I simply do not understand what has happened. . . . Where are those detectives? . . . Will no one explain? . . . *You*

141

treat me like a child," he said. It was all like one of those Cabinet meetings, when they all talked about something he didn't understand and paid no attention to him.

Father Rothschild led him away, and attempted with almost humiliating patience and tact to make clear to him some of the complexities of modern journalism.

"I don't believe a word of it," the Prime Minister kept saying. "It's all humbug. You're keeping something back. . . . *Chatterbox,* indeed."

Simon Balcairn was given his hat and coat and shown to the door. The crowd round the awning had dispersed. It was still raining. He walked back to his little flat in Bourdon Street. The rain washed a few of the remaining locks from his face; it dripped down his collar.

They were washing a car outside his front door; he crept between it and his dustbin, fitted his latchkey in the lock and went upstairs. His flat was like *Chez Espinosa*—all oilcloth and Lalique glass; there were some enterprising photographs by David Lennox, a gramophone (on the instalment system) and numberless cards of invitation on the mantelpiece. His bath towel was where he had left it on his bed.

Simon went to the ice box in the kitchen and chipped off some ice. Then he made himself a cocktail. Then he went to the telephone.

"Central ten thousand . . ." he said. ". . . Give me Mrs. Brace. Hullo, this is Balcairn."

"Well . . . gotcher story?"

"Oh yes, I've got my story, only this isn't gossip, it's news—front page. You'll have to fill up the Chatterbox page on Espinosa's."

"Hell!"

"Wait till you see the story. . . . Hullo, give me news, will you. . . . This is Balcairn. Put on one of the boys to take this down, will you? . . . Ready? All right."

At his glass-topped table, sipping his cocktail, Simon Balcairn dictated his last story.

"Scenes of wild religious enthusiasm, comma, reminiscent of a negro camp-meeting in Southern America, comma, broke out in the heart of Mayfair yesterday evening at the party given for the famous American Revivalist Mrs. Ape by the Viscountess Metroland, formerly the Hon. Mrs. Beste-Chetwynd, at her historic mansion, Pastmaster House, stop. The magnificent ballroom can never have enshrined a more brilliant assembly . . ."

143

It was his swan-song. Lie after monstrous lie bubbled up in his brain.

"*. . . The Hon. Agatha Runcible joined Mrs. Ape among the orchids and led the singing, tears coursing down her face. . . .*"

Excitement spread at the *Excess* office. The machines were stopped. The night staff of reporters, slightly tipsy, as always at that hour, stood over the stenographer as he typed. The compositors snatched the sheets of copy as they came. The sub-editors began ruthlessly cutting and scrapping; they suppressed important political announcements, garbled the evidence at a murder trial, reduced the dramatic criticism to one caustic paragraph, to make room for Simon's story.

It came through "hot and strong, as nice as mother makes it," as one of them remarked.

"Little Lord Fauntleroy's on a good thing at last," said another.

"What-ho," said a third appreciatively.

"*. . . barely had Lady Everyman finished before the Countess of Throbbing rose to confess her sins, and in a voice broken with emotion disclosed the hitherto unverified details of the parentage of the present Earl. . . .*"

"Tell Mr. Edwards to look up photographs of all three of 'em," said the assistant news editor.

". . . *The Marquess of Vanburgh shaken by sobs of contrition. . . . Mrs. Panrast, singing feverishly. . . . Lady Anchorage with downcast eyes.*

". . . *The Archbishop of Canterbury, who up to now had remained unmoved by the general emotion, then testified that at Eton in the 'eighties he and Sir James Brown . . .*

". . . *The Duchess of Stayle next threw down her emerald and diamond tiara, crying 'a Guilt Offering,' an example which was quickly followed by the Countess of Circumference and Lady Brown, until a veritable rain of precious stones fell on to the parquet flooring, heirlooms of priceless value rolling among Tecla pearls and Chanel diamonds. A blank cheque fluttered from the hands of the Maharajah of Pukkapore . . .*"

It made over two columns, and when Simon finally rang off, after receiving the congratulations of his colleagues, he was for the first time in his journalistic experience perfectly happy about his work. He finished the watery dregs of the cocktail shaker and went into the kitchen. He shut the door and the window and opened the door of the gas-oven. Inside it was very

145

black and dirty and smelled of meat. He spread a sheet of newspaper on the lowest tray and lay down, resting his head on it. Then he noticed that by some mischance he had chosen Vanburgh's gossip-page in the *Morning Despatch*. He put in another sheet. (There were crumbs on the floor.) Then he turned on the gas. It came surprisingly with a loud roar; the wind of it stirred his hair and the remaining particles of his beard. At first he held his breath. Then he thought that was silly and gave a sniff. The sniff made him cough, and coughing made him breathe, and breathing made him feel very ill; but soon he fell into a coma and presently died.

So the last Earl of Balcairn went, as they say, to his fathers (who had fallen in many lands and for many causes, as the eccentricities of British Foreign Policy and their own wandering natures had directed them; at Acre and Agincourt and Killiecrankie, in Egypt and America. One had been picked white by fishes as the tides rolled him among the tree-tops of a submarine forest; some had grown black and unfit for consideration under tropical suns; while many of them lay in marble tombs of extravagant design).

146

At Pastmaster House, Lady Metroland and Lord Monomark were talking about him. Lord Monomark was roaring with boyish laughter.

"That's a great lad," he said. "Came in a false beard, did he? That's peppy. What'd you say his name was? I'll raise him tomorrow first thing."

And he turned to give Simon's name to an attendant secretary.

And when Lady Metroland began to expostulate, he shut her up rather discourteously.

"Shucks, Margot," he said. "You know better than to get on a high horse with me."

VII

HEN Adam became Mr. Chatterbox. He and Nina were lunching at Espinosa's and quarrelling half-heartedly when a business-like, Eton-cropped woman came across to their table, whom Adam recognized as the social editress of the *Daily Excess*.

"See here," she said, "weren't you over at the office with Balcairn the day he did himself in?"

"Yes."

"Well, a pretty mess he's let us in for. Sixty-two writs for libel up to date and more coming in. And that's not the worst. Left me to do his job and mine. I was wondering if you could tell me the names of any of these people and anything about them."

Adam pointed out a few well-worn faces.

"Yes, they ain't no good. They're on the black list. You see, Monomark was in an awful way about Balcairn's story of Lady Metroland's party, and he's sent down a chit that none of the people who're bringing actions against the paper can be mentioned again. Well, I ask you, what's one to do? It's just bricks without straw. Why, we can't even mention the Prime Minister or the Archbishop of Canterbury. I suppose you don't know of anyone who'd care to take on the job? They'd have to be a pretty good mutt, if they would."

"What do they pay?"

"Ten pounds a week and expenses. Know anyone?"

"I'd do it myself for that."

"You?" The social editress looked at him sceptically. "Would you be any good?"

"I'll try for a week or two."

"That's about as long as anyone sticks it. All right, come back to the office with me when you've finished lunch. You can't cause more trouble than Balcairn, anyhow, and he looked the goods at first."

"Now we can get married," said Nina.

Meanwhile the libel actions against the authors, printers and publishers of Simon Balcairn's last story practically paralysed the judicial system of the country. The old brigade, led by Mrs. Blackwater, threw themselves with relish into an orgy of litigation such as they had not seen since the war (one of the younger counsel causing Lady Throbbing particular delight. . . . "I do think, when you get to my age, dear, there is something *sympathique* about a wig, don't you? . . ."). The younger generation for the most part allowed their cases to be settled out of court and later gave a very delightful party on the proceeds in a captive dirigible. Miss Runcible, less well advised, filled two albums with Press cuttings portraying her various appearances at the Law Courts, sometimes as plaintiff, sometimes as witness, sometimes (in a hat borrowed from Miss Mouse) as part of the queue of "fashionably dressed women waiting for admission," once as an intruder being removed by an usher from the Press gallery, and finally as prisoner being sentenced to a fine of ten pounds or seven days' imprisonment for contempt of court.

The proceedings were considerably complicated by the behaviour of Mrs. Ape, who gave an interview in which she fully confirmed Simon Balcairn's story. She also caused her Press agent to wire a further account to all parts of the world. She then left the country with her angels, having received a sudden call to ginger up the religious life of Oberammergau.

At intervals letters arrived from Buenos Aires in which Chastity and Divine Discontent spoke rather critically of Latin American entertainment.

"They didn't know when they was well off," said Mrs. Ape.

"It don't sound much different from us," said Creative Endeavour wistfully.

"They won't be dead five minutes before *they* see the difference," said Mrs. Ape.

Edward Throbbing and two secretaries returned to Hertford Street somewhat inopportunely for Miles and his dirt-track racer, who were obliged to move into Shepheard's. Miles said that the thing he resented about his brother's return was not so much the inconvenience as the expense. For some weeks Throbbing suffered from the successive discoveries by his secretaries of curious and compromising things in all parts of the house; his butler, too, seemed changed. He hiccoughed heavily while serving dinner to two Secretaries of State, complained of spiders in his bath and the sound of musical instruments, and finally had "the horrors," ran mildly amok in the pantry with the kitchen poker, and had to be taken away in a van. Long after these immediate causes of distress had been removed, the life of Throbbing's secretaries was

151

periodically disturbed by ambiguous telephone calls and the visits of menacing young men who wanted new suits or tickets to America, or a fiver to go on with.

But all these events, though of wide general interest, are of necessity a closed book to the readers of Mr. Chatterbox's page.

Lord Monomark's black list had made a devastating change in the personnel of the *Daily Excess* gossip. In a single day Mr. Chatterbox's readers found themselves plunged into a murky underworld of nonentities. They were shown photographs of the misshapen daughters of backwoods peers carrying buckets of meal to their fathers' chickens; they learned of the engagement of the younger sister of the Bishop of Chertsey and of a dinner party given in Elm Park Gardens by the widow of a High Commissioner to some of the friends she had made in their colony. There were details of the blameless home life of women novelists, photographed with their spaniels before rose-covered cottages; stories of undergraduate "rags" and regimental reunion dinners; anecdotes from Harley Street and the Inns of Court; snaps and snippets about cocktail parties given in basement flats by spotty announcers at the B.B.C., of tea dances in Gloucester Terrace and jokes made at High Table by dons.

Urged on by the taunts of the social editress, Adam brought new enterprise and humanity into this sorry column. He started a series of "Notable Invalids," which was, from the first, wildly successful. He began chattily. *"At a dinner party the other evening, my neighbour and I began to compile a list of the most popular deaf peeresses. First, of course, came old Lady —— . . ."*

Next day he followed it up with a page about deaf peers and statesmen, then about the one-legged, blind and bald. Postcards of appreciation poured in from all over the country.

"I have read your column for many years now," wrote a correspondent from Bude, *"but this is the first time I have really enjoyed it. I have myself been deaf for a long time, and it is a great comfort to me to know that my affliction is shared by so many famous men and women. Thank you, Mr. Chatterbox, and good luck to you."*

Another wrote: *"Ever since childhood I have been cursed with abnormally large ears which have been a source of ridicule to me and a serious handicap in my career (I am a chub fuddler). I should be so glad to*

153

know whether any great people have suffered in the same way."

Finally, he ransacked the lunatic asylums and mental houses of the country, and for nearly a week ran an extremely popular series under the heading of "Titled Eccentrics."

"It is not generally known that the Earl of ——, who lives in strict retirement, has the unusual foible of wearing costume of the Napoleonic Period. So great, indeed, is his detestation of modern dress that on one occasion . . ."

"Lord ——, whose public appearances are regrettably rare nowadays, is a close student of comparative religions. There is an amusing story of how, when lunching with the then Dean of Westminster, Lord —— startled his host by proclaiming that so far from being of divine ordinance, the Ten Commandments were, in point of fact, composed by himself and delivered by him to Moses on Sinai. . . ."

"Lady ——, whose imitations of animal sounds are so life-like that she can seldom be persuaded to converse in any other way . . ."

And so on.

Besides this, arguing that people did not really mind *whom* they read about provided that a kind of vicarious inquisitiveness into the lives of others was satisfied, Adam began to invent people.

He invented a sculptor called Provna, the son of a Polish nobleman, who lived in a top-floor studio in Grosvenor House. Most of his work (which was all in private hands) was constructed in cork, vulcanite and steel. The Metropolitan Museum at New York, Mr. Chatterbox learned, had been negotiating for some time to purchase a specimen, but so far had been unable to outbid the collectors.

Such is the power of the Press, that soon after this a steady output of early Provnas began to travel from Warsaw to Bond Street and from Bond Street to California, while Mrs. Hoop announced to her friends that Provna was at the moment at work on a bust of Johnny, which she intended to present to the nation (a statement which Adam was unable to record owing to the presence of Mrs. Hoop's name on the black list, but which duly appeared, under a photograph of Johnny, in the Marquess of Vanburgh's rival column).

Encouraged by his success, Adam began gradually to introduce to his readers a brilliant and lovely company. He mentioned them casually at first in lists of genuine people. There was a popular young attaché

155

at the Italian Embassy called Count Cincinnati. He was descended from the famous Roman Consul, Cincinnatus, and bore a plough as his crest. Count Cincinnati was held to be the best amateur 'cellist in London. Adam saw him one evening dancing at the Café de la Paix. A few evenings later Lord Vanburgh noticed him at Covent Garden, remarking that his collection of the original designs for the Russian ballet was unequalled in Europe. Two days later Adam sent him to Monte Carlo for a few days' rest, and Vanburgh hinted that there was more in this visit than met the eye, and mentioned the daughter of a well-known American hostess who was staying there at her aunt's villa.

There was a Captain Angus Stuart-Kerr, too, whose rare appearances in England were a delight to his friends; unlike most big-game hunters, he was an expert and indefatigable dancer. Much to Adam's disgust he found Captain Stuart-Kerr taken up by an unknown gossip-writer in a two-penny illustrated weekly, who saw him at a point-to-point meeting, and remarked that he was well known as the hardest rider in the Hebrides. Adam put a stop to that next day.

"Some people," he wrote, *"are under the impression that Captain Angus Stuart-Kerr, whom I mentioned*
156

on this page a short time ago, is a keen rider. Perhaps they are confusing him with Alastair Kerr-Stuart, of Inverauchty, a very distant cousin. Captain Stuart-Kerr never rides, and for a very interesting reason. There is an old Gaelic rhyme repeated among his clansmen which says in rough translation 'the Laird rides well on two legs.' Tradition has it that when the head of the house mounts a horse the clan will be dispersed." *

But Adam's most important creation was Mrs. Andrew Quest. There was always some difficulty about introducing English people into his column as his readers had a way of verifying his references in Debrett (as he knew to his cost, for one day, having referred to the engagement of the third and youngest daughter of a Welsh baronet, he received six postcards, eighteen telephone calls, a telegram and a personal visit of protest to inform him that there are two equally beautiful sisters still in the schoolroom. The social editress had been scathing about this.) However, he put Imogen Quest down one day, quietly and

* This story, slightly expanded, found its way later into a volume of Highland Legends called *Tales from the Mist*, which has been approved to be read in elementary schools. This shows the difference between what is called a "living" as opposed to a "dead" folk tradition.

157

decisively, as the most lovely and popular of the younger married set. And from the first she exhibited signs of a marked personality. Adam wisely eschewed any attempts at derivation, but his readers nodded to each other and speedily supplied her with an exalted if irregular origin. Everything else Adam showered upon her. She had slightly more than average height, and was very dark and slim, with large Laurencin eyes and the negligent grace of the trained athlete (she fenced with the sabre for half an hour every morning before breakfast). Even Provna, who was notoriously indifferent to conventional beauty, described her as "justifying the century."

Her clothes were incomparable, with just that suggestion of the haphazard which raised them high above the mere *chic* of the mannequin.

Her character was a lovely harmony of contending virtues—she was witty and tender-hearted; passionate and serene, sensual and temperate, impulsive and discreet.

Her set, the most intimate and brilliant in Europe, achieved a superb mean between those two poles of savagery Lady Circumstance and Lady Metroland.

Soon Imogen Quest became a byword for social inaccessibility—the final goal for all climbers.

Adam went one day to a shop in Hanover Square to watch Nina buy some hats and was seriously incommoded by the heaps of bandboxes disposed on the chairs and dressing-tables ostentatiously addressed to Mrs. Andrew Quest. He could hear her name spoken reverently in cocktail clubs, and casually let slip in such phrases as "My dear, I never see Peter now. He spends all his time with Imogen Quest," or "As Imogen would say . . ." or "I think the Quests have got one like that. I must ask them where it came from." And this knowledge on the intangible Quest set, moving among them in uncontrolled dignity of life, seemed to leaven and sweeten the lives of Mr. Chatterbox's readers.

One day Imogen gave a party, the preparations for which occupied several paragraphs. On the following day Adam found his table deep in letters of complaint from gate-crashers who had found the house in Seamore Place untenanted.

Finally a message came down that Lord Monomark was interested in Mrs. Quest; could Mr. Chatterbox arrange a meeting. That day the Quests sailed for Jamaica.

Adam also attempted in an unobtrusive way to exercise some influence over the clothes of his readers.

"I noticed at the Café de la Paix yesterday evening," he wrote, *"that two of the smartest men in the room were wearing black suède shoes with their evening clothes—one of them, who shall be nameless, was a Very Important Person indeed. I hear that this fashion, which comes, like so many others, from New York, is likely to become popular over here this season."* A few days later he mentioned Captain Kerr-Stuart's appearance at the Embassy *"wearing, of course, the ultra-fashionable black suède shoes."* In a week he was gratified to notice that Johnny Hoop and Archie Schwert had both followed Captain Stuart-Kerr's lead, while in a fortnight the big emporiums of ready-made clothes in Regent Street had transposed their tickets in the windows and arranged rows of black suède shoes on a silver step labelled "For evening wear."

His attempt to introduce a bottle-green bowler hat, however, was not successful; in fact, a "well-known St. James's Street hatter," when interviewed by an evening paper on the subject, said that he had never seen or heard of such a thing, and though he would not refuse to construct one if requested to by an old customer, he was of the opinion that no old customer of his would require a hat of that kind (though there

160

was a sad case of an impoverished old beau who attempted to stain a grey hat with green ink, as once in years gone by he had been used to dye the carnation for his buttonhole).

As the days passed, Mr. Chatterbox's page became almost wholly misleading. With sultanesque caprice Adam would tell his readers of inaccessible eating-houses which were now the centre of fashion; he drove them to dance in temperance hotels in Bloomsbury. In a paragraph headed "Montparnasse in Belgravia," he announced that the buffet at Sloane Square tube station had become the haunt of the most modern artistic coterie (Mr. Benfleet hurried there on his first free evening, but saw no one but Mrs. Hoop and Lord Vanburgh and a plebeian toper with a celluloid collar).

As a last resort, on those hopeless afternoons when invention failed and that black misanthropy settled on him which waits alike on gossip writer and novelist, Adam sometimes found consolation in seizing upon some gentle and self-effacing citizen and transfiguring him with a blaze of notoriety.

He did this with a man called Ginger.

As part of his duties, which led him into many unusual places, Adam and Nina went up to Manchester for the November Handicap. Here they had the disheartening experience of seeing Indian Runner come in an easy winner and the totalizator paying out thirty-five to one. It was during the bottle-green bowler campaign, and Adam was searching in vain for any sign of his influence when, suddenly, among the crowd, he saw the genial red face of the drunk major to whom he had entrusted his thousand pounds at Lottie's. It seemed odd that a man so bulky could be so elusive. Adam was not sure whether the Major saw him, but in some mysterious way Adam's pursuit coincided with the Major's complete disappearance. The crowd became very dense, brandishing flasks and sandwiches. When Adam reached the spot where the Major had stood he found two policemen arresting a pickpocket.

" 'Ere, who are you pushing?" asked the spectators.

"Have you seen a drunk major anywhere?" asked Adam.

But no one could help him, and he returned disconsolately to Nina, whom he found in conversation with a young man with a curly red moustache.

The young man said he was fed up with racing, and Adam said he was too; so the young man said why didn't they come back to London in his bus, so Adam and Nina said they would. The bus turned out to be a very large, brand-new racing car, and they got to London in time for dinner. Nina explained that the young man used to play with her as a child, and that he had been doing something military in Ceylon for the last five years. The young man's name was Eddy Littlejohn, but over dinner he said, look here, would they call him Ginger; everyone else did. So they began to call him Ginger, and he said wouldn't it be a good idea if they had another bottle of fizz, and Nina and Adam said yes, it would, so they had a magnum and got very friendly.

"You know," said Ginger, "it was awful luck meeting you two today. I was getting awfully fed up with London. It's so damn slow. I came back meaning to have a good time, you know, paint the place a bit red, and all that. Well, the other day I was reading the paper, and there was a bit that said that the posh place to go to dance nowadays was the Casanova Hotel in Bloomsbury. Well, it seemed a bit rum to me—place I'd never heard of, you know—but, still, I'd been away for some time and places change and all that, so I put on my bib and tucker and toddled off, hoping for a bit of innocent amusement. Well, I mean to say,

163

you never saw such a place. There were only about three people dancing, so I said, 'Where's the bar?' And they said, 'Bar!' And I said, 'You know, for a drink.' And they said, well, they could probably make me some coffee. And I said, 'No, not coffee.' And then they said they hadn't got a licence for what they called alcohol. Well, I mean to say, if that's the best London can do, give me Colombo. I wonder who writes things like that in the papers?"

"As a matter of fact, *I* do."

"I say no, do you? You must be frightfully brainy. Did you write all that about the green bowlers?"

"Yes."

"Well, I mean to say, whoever heard of a green bowler, I mean. . . . I tell you what, you know, I believe it was all a leg pull. You know, I think that's damn funny. Why, a whole lot of poor mutts may have gone and bought green bowlers."

After this they went on to the Café de la Paix, where they met Johnny Hoop, who asked them all to the party in a few days' time in the captive balloon.

But Ginger was not to be had twice.

"Oh, no, you know," he said, "not in a captive balloon. You're trying to pull the old leg again. Whoever heard of a party in a captive balloon? I mean to say, suppose one fell out, I mean?"

Adam telephoned his page through to the *Excess*, and soon after this a coloured singer appeared, paddling his black suède shoes in a pool of limelight, who excited Ginger's disapproval. He didn't mind niggers, Ginger said; remarking justly that niggers were all very well in their place, but, after all, one didn't come all the way from Colombo to London just to see niggers. So they left the Café de la Paix, and went to Lottie's, where Ginger became a little moody, saying that London wasn't home to him any more and that things were changed.

"You know," said Ginger, "all the time I've been out in Ceylon I've always said to myself, 'As soon as the governor kicks the bucket, and I come in for the family doubloons and pieces of eight, I'm going to come back to England and have a real old bust.' And now when it comes to the point there doesn't seem to be anything I much want to do."

"How about a little drink?" said Lottie.

So Ginger had a drink, and then he and an American sang the Eton Boating Song several times. At the end of the evening he admitted that there was some life left in the jolly old capital of the Empire.

Next day Mr. Chatterbox's readers learned that: *"Captain 'Ginger' Littlejohn, as he is known to his intimates, was one of the well-known sporting figures at the November Handicap who favoured the new bottle-green bowler. Captain Littlejohn is one of the wealthiest and best-known bachelors in Society, and I have lately heard his name spoken of in connection with the marriage of the daughter of a famous ducal house. He came all the way to yesterday's races in his own motor omnibus, which he drives himself . . ."*

For some days Ginger's name figured largely on Adam's page, to his profound embarrassment. Several engagements were predicted for him, it was rumoured that he had signed a contract with a film company, that he had bought a small island in the Bristol Channel which he proposed to turn into a country club, and that his forthcoming novel about Singalese life contained many very thinly disguised portraits of London celebrities.

But the green-bowler joke had gone too far. Adam was sent for by Lord Monomark.

"Now see here, Symes," said the great man, "I like your page. It's peppy, it's got plenty of new names in it and it's got the intimate touch I like. I read it every day and so does my daughter. Keep on that

166

way and you'll be all right. But *what's all this about bottle-green bowlers?*"

"Well, of course, sir, they're only worn by a limited number of people at present, but . . ."

"Have you got one? Show me a green bowler."

"I don't wear one myself, I'm afraid."

"Well, where d'you see 'em? I haven't seen one yet. My daughter hasn't seen one. Who does wear 'em? Where do they buy 'em? That's what I want to know. Now see here, Symes, I don't say that there ain't any such thing as a green bowler; there may be and again there mayn't. But from now on there are going to be no more bottle-green bowlers in my paper. See. And another thing. This Count Cincinnati. I don't say *he* doesn't exist. He may do and he mayn't. But the Italian Ambassador doesn't know anything about him and the Almanak de Gotha doesn't. So as far as my paper goes that's good enough for him. And I don't want any more about Espinosa's. They made out my bill wrong last night.

"Got those three things clear? Tabulate them in the mind—1, 2, 3, that's the secret of memory. Tab-u-late. All right, then, run along now and tell the Home Secretary he can come right in. You'll find him waiting in the passage—ugly little man with pince-nez."

VIII

WO nights later Adam and Nina took Ginger to the party in the captive dirigible. It was not a really good evening. The long drive in Ginger's car to the degraded suburb where the airship was moored chilled and depressed them, dissipating the gaiety which had flickered rather spasmodically over Ginger's dinner.

The airship seemed to fill the whole field, tethered a few feet from the ground by innumerable cables over which they stumbled painfully on the way to the steps. These had been covered by a socially minded caterer with a strip of red carpet.

Inside the saloons were narrow and hot, communicating to each other by spiral staircases and metal alleys. There were protrusions at every corner, and Miss Runcible had made herself a mass of bruises in the first half hour. There was a band and a bar and a

168

all the same faces. It was the first time that a party was given in an airship.

Adam went aloft to a kind of terrace. Acres of inflated silk blotted out the sky, stirring just perceptibly in the breeze. The lights of other cars arriving lit up the uneven grass. A few louts had collected round the gates to jeer. There were two people making love to each other near him on the terrace, reclining on cushions. There was also a young woman he did not know, holding one of the stays and breathing heavily; evidently she felt unwell. One of the lovers lit a cigar and Adam observed that they were Mary Mouse and the Maharajah of Pukkapore.

Presently Nina joined him. "It seems such a waste," she said, thinking of Mary and the Maharajah, "that two very rich people like that should fall in love with each other."

"Nina," said Adam, "let's get married soon, don't you think?"

"Yes, it's a bore not being married."

The young woman who felt ill passed by them, walking shakily, to try and find her coat and her young man to take her home.

". . . I don't know if it sounds absurd," said Adam, "but I do feel that a marriage ought to *go on*—for quite a long time, I mean. D'you feel that too, at all?"

"Yes, it's one of the things about a marriage!"

"I'm glad you feel that. I didn't quite know if you did. Otherwise it's all rather bogus, isn't it?"

"I think you ought to go and see papa again," said Nina. "It's never any good writing. Go and tell him that you've got a job and are terribly rich and that we're going to be married before Christmas!"

"All right. I'll do that."

". . . D'you remember last month we arranged for you to go and see him the first time? . . . just like this . . . it was at Archie Schwert's party . . ."

"Oh, Nina, *what a lot of parties.*"

(. . . Masked parties, Savage parties, Victorian parties, Greek parties, Wild West parties, Russian parties, Circus parties, parties where one had to dress as somebody else, almost naked parties in St. John's Wood, parties in flats and studios and houses and ships and hotels and night clubs, in windmills and swimming baths, tea parties at school where one ate muffins and meringues and tinned crab, parties at Oxford where one drank brown sherry and smoked Turkish cigarettes, dull dances in London and comic dances in Scotland and disgusting dances in Paris—
170

all that succession and repetition of massed humanity. . . . Those vile bodies . . .)

He leant his forehead, to cool it, on Nina's arm and
kissed her in the hollow of her forearm.

"*I know,* darling," she said and put her hand on his
hair.

Ginger came strutting jauntily by, his hands clasped
under his coat-tails.

"Hullo, you two," he said. "Pretty good show this,
what!"

"Are you enjoying yourself, Ginger?"

"*Rather.* I say, I've met an awful good chap called
Miles. Regular topper. You know, *pally.* That's what
I like about a really decent party—you meet such
topping fellows. I mean some chaps it takes absolutely
years to know, but a chap like Miles I feel is a pal
straight away."

Presently cars began to drive away again. Miss
Runcible said that she had heard of a divine night
club near Leicester Square somewhere where you could
get a drink at any hour of the night. It was called the
St. Christopher's Social Club.

So they all went there in Ginger's car.

On the way Ginger said, "That cove Miles, you
know, he's awfully *queer* . . ."

171

St. Christopher's Social Club took some time to find.

It was a little door at the side of a shop, and the man who opened it held his foot against it and peeped round.

They paid ten shillings each and signed false names in the visitors' book. Then they went downstairs to a very hot room full of cigarette smoke; there were unsteady tables with bamboo legs round the walls and there were some people in shirt sleeves dancing on a shiny linoleum floor.

There was a woman in a yellow beaded frock playing a piano and another in red playing the fiddle.

They ordered some whisky. The waiter said he was sorry, but he couldn't oblige, not that night he couldn't. The police had just rung up to say that they were going to make a raid any minute. If they liked they could have some nice kippers.

Miss Runcible said that kippers were not very drunk-making and that the whole club seemed bogus to her.

Ginger said well anyway they had better have some kippers now they were there. Then he asked Nina to dance and she said no. Then he asked Miss Runcible and she said no, too.

172

Then they ate kippers.

Presently one of the men in shirt sleeves (who had clearly had a lot to drink before the St. Christopher Social Club knew about the police) came up to their table and said to Adam:—

"You don't know me. I'm Gilmour. I don't want to start a row in front of ladies, but when I see a howling cad I like to tell him so."

Adam said, "Why do you spit when you talk?"

Gilmour said, "That is a very unfortunate physical disability, and it shows what a howling cad you are that you mention it."

Then Ginger said, "Same to you, old boy, with nobs on."

Then Gilmour said, "Hullo, Ginger, old scout."

And Ginger said, "Why, it's Bill. You mustn't mind Bill. Awfully stout chap. Met him on the boat."

Gilmour said, "Any pal of Ginger's is a pal of mine."

So Adam and Gilmour shook hands.

Gilmour said, "This is a pretty low joint, anyhow. You chaps come round to my place and have a drink."

So they went to Gilmour's place.

Gilmour's place was a bed–sitting-room in Ryder Street.

So they sat on the bed in Gilmour's place and drank whisky while Gilmour was sick next door.

And Ginger said, "There's nowhere like London really you know."

That same evening while Adam and Nina sat on the deck of the dirigible a party of quite a different sort was being given at Anchorage House. This last survivor of the noble town houses of London was, in its time, of dominating and august dimensions, and even now, when it had become a mere "picturesque bit" lurking in a ravine between concrete skyscrapers, its pillared façade, standing back from the street and obscured by railings and some wisps of foliage, had grace and dignity and other-worldliness enough to cause a flutter or two in Mrs. Hoop's heart as she drove into the forecourt.

"Can't you just see the *ghosts?*" she said to Lady Circumference on the stairs. "Pitt and Fox and Burke and Lady Hamilton and Beau Brummel and Dr. Johnson" (a concurrence of celebrities, it may be remarked, at which something memorable might surely have occurred). "Can't you just *see* them—in their buckled shoes?"

Lady Circumference raised her lorgnette and surveyed the stream of guests debouching from the cloak-rooms like City workers from the Underground. She saw Mr. Outrage and Lord Metroland in consultation about the Censorship Bill (a statesmanlike and much-needed measure which empowered a committee of five atheists to destroy all books, pictures and films they considered undesirable, without any nonsense about defence or appeal). She saw both Archbishops, the Duke and Duchess of Stayle, Lord Vanburgh and Lady Metroland, Lady Throbbing and Edward Throbbing and Mrs. Blackwater, Mrs. Mouse and Lord Monomark and a superb Levantine, and behind and about them a great concourse of pious and honourable people (many of whom made the Anchorage House reception the one outing of the year), their women-folk well gowned in rich and durable stuffs, their men-folk ablaze with orders; people who had represented their country in foreign places and sent their sons to die for her in battle, people of decent and temperate life, uncultured, unaffected, unembarrassed, unassuming, unambitious people, of independent judgment and marked eccentricities, kind people who cared for animals and the deserving poor, brave and rather unreasonable people, that fine phalanx of the passing order, approaching, as one day at the Last

Trump they hoped to meet their Maker, with decorous and frank cordiality to shake Lady Anchorage by the hand at the top of her staircase. Lady Circumference saw all this and sniffed the exhalation of her own herd. But she saw no ghosts.

"That's all my eye," she said.

But Mrs. Hoop ascended step by step in a confused but very glorious dream of eighteenth-century elegance.

The Presence of Royalty was heavy as thunder in the drawing-room.

The Baroness Yoshiwara and the Prime Minister met once more.

"I tried to see you twice this week," she said, "but always you were busy. We are leaving London. Perhaps you heard? My husband has been moved to Washington. It was his wish to go . . ."

"No. I say, Baroness . . . I had no idea. That's very bad news. We shall all miss you terribly."

"I thought perhaps I would come to make my adieux. One day next week."

"Why, yes, of course, that would be delightful. You must both come to dine. I'll get my secretary to fix something up tomorrow."

"It has been nice being in London . . . you were kind."

"Not a bit. I don't know what London could be without our guests from abroad."

"Oh, twenty damns to your great pig-face," said the Baroness suddenly and turned away.

Mr. Outrage watched her bewildered. Finally he said, "For East is East and West is West and never the twain shall meet" (which was a poor conclusion for a former Foreign Secretary).

Edward Throbbing stood talking to the eldest daughter of the Duchess of Stayle. She was some inches taller than he and inclined slightly so that, in the general murmur of conversation, she should not miss any of his colonial experiences. She wore a frock such as only Duchesses can obtain for their elder daughters, a garment curiously puckered and puffed up and enriched with old lace at improbable places, from which her pale beauty emerged as though from a clumsily tied parcel. Neither powder, rouge nor lipstick had played any part in her toilet and her colourless hair was worn long and bound across her forehead in a broad fillet. Long pearl drops hung from her ears and she wore a tight little collar of pearls round

177

her throat. It was generally understood that now Edward Throbbing was back these two would become engaged to be married.

Lady Ursula was acquiescent if unenthusiastic. When she thought about marriage at all, which was rarely (for her chief interests were a girls' club in Canning Town and a younger brother at school), she thought what a pity it was that one had to be so ill to have children. Her married friends spoke of this almost with relish and her mother with awe.

An innate dilatoriness of character rather than any doubt of the ultimate issue kept Edward from verbal proposal. He had decided to arrange everything before Christmas and that was enough. He had no doubt that a suitable occasion would soon be devised for him. It was clearly suitable that he should marry before he was thirty. Now and then when he was with Ursula he felt a slight quickening of possessive impulse towards her fragility and distance; occasionally when he read some rather lubricious novel or saw much love-making on the stage he would translate the characters in his mind and put Lady Ursula, often incongruously, in the place of the heroine. He had no doubt that he was in love. Perhaps he would propose this very evening and get it over. It was up to Lady

178

Ursula to engineer an occasion. Meanwhile he kept the conversation on to the subject of labour problems in Montreal, about which his information was extensive and accurate.

"He's a nice, steady boy," said the Duchess, "and it's a comfort, nowadays, to see two young people so genuinely fond of each other. Of course, nothing is actually arranged yet, but I was talking to Fanny Throbbing yesterday, and apparently Edward has already spoken to her on the subject. I think that everything will be settled before Christmas. Of course, there's not a great deal of money, but one's learnt not to expect that nowadays, and Mr. Outrage speaks very highly of his ability. Quite one of the coming men in the party."

"Well," said Lady Circumference, "you know your own business, but if you ask me I shouldn't care to see a daughter of mine marry into that family. Bad hats every one of them. Look at the father and the sister, and from all I hear the brother is rotten all through."

"I don't say it's a match I should have chosen myself. There's certainly a bad strain in the Malpractices . . . but you know how headstrong children are nowadays, and they seem so fond of each other . . .

and there seem so few young men about. At least I never seem to see any."

"Young toads, the whole lot of them," said Lady Circumference.

"And these *terrible* parties which I'm told they give. I don't know what I should have done if Ursula had ever wanted to go to them . . . the poor Chasms. . . ."

"If I were Viola Chasm I'd give that girl a thunderin' good hidin'."

The topic of the Younger Generation spread through the company like a yawn. Royalty remarked on their absence and those happy mothers who had even one docile daughter in tow swelled with pride and commiseration.

"I'm told that they're having another of their parties," said Mrs. Mouse, "in an aeroplane this time."

"In an aeroplane? How very extraordinary."

"Of course, I never hear a word from Mary, but her maid told my maid . . ."

"What I always wonder, Kitty dear, is what they actually *do* at these parties of theirs. I mean, *do* they . . . ?"

180

"My dear, from all I hear, I think they do."

"Oh, to be young again, Kitty. When I think, my dear, of all the trouble and exertion which we had to go through to be even moderately bad . . . those passages in the early morning and mama sleeping next door."

"And yet, my dear, I doubt very much whether they really *appreciate* it all as much as we should . . . young people take things so much for granted."

"*Si la jeunesse savait*, Kitty . . ."

"*Si la vieillesse pouvait.*"

Later that evening Mr. Outrage stood almost alone in the supper-room drinking a glass of champagne. Another episode in his life was closed, another of those tantalizing glimpses of felicity capriciously withdrawn. Poor Mr. Outrage, thought Mr. Outrage; poor, poor old Outrage, always just on the verge of revelation, of some sublime and transfiguring experience; always frustrated. . . . Just Prime Minister, nothing more, bullied by his colleagues, a source of income to low caricaturists. Was Mr. Outrage an immortal soul, thought Mr. Outrage; had he wings, was he free and unconfined, was he born for eternity? He sipped his

181

champagne, fingered his ribbon of the Garter, and resigned himself to the dust.

Presently he was joined by Lord Metroland and Father Rothschild.

"Margot's left—gone on to some party in an airship. I've been talking to Lady Anchorage for nearly an hour about the younger generation."

"Everyone seems to have been talking about the younger generation tonight. The most boring subject I know."

"Well, after all, what does all this stand for if there's going to be no one to carry it on?"

"All what?" Mr. Outrage looked round the supper-room, deserted save for two footmen who leant against the walls looking as waxen as the clumps of flowers sent up that morning from hothouses in the country. "What does all what stand for?"

"All this business of government."

"As far as I'm concerned it stands for a damned lot of hard work and precious little in return. If those young people can find a way to get on without it, good luck to them."

"I see what Metroland means," said Father Rothschild.

"Blessed if I do. Anyway I've got no children myself, and I'm thankful for it. I don't understand them, and I don't want to. They had a chance after the war that no generation has ever had. There was a whole civilization to be saved and remade—and all they seem to do is to play the fool. Mind you, I'm all in favour of them having a fling. I dare say that Victorian ideas *were* a bit strait-laced. Saving your cloth, Rothschild, it's only human nature to run a bit loose when one's young. But there's something wanton about these young people today. That stepson of yours, Metroland, and that girl of poor old Chasm's and young Throbbing's brother."

"Don't you think," said Father Rothschild gently, "that perhaps it is all in some way historical? I don't think people ever *want* to lose their faith either in religion or anything else. I know very few young people, but it seems to me that they are all possessed with an almost fatal hunger for permanence. I think all these divorces show that. People aren't content just to muddle along nowadays. . . . And this word 'bogus' they all use. . . . They won't make the best of a bad job nowadays. My private schoolmaster used to say, 'If a thing's worth doing at all, it's worth doing well.' My Church has taught that in different words for several centuries. But these young people have got hold of another end of the stick, and for all we know it may be the right one. They say, 'If a thing's not worth doing well, it's not worth doing at all.' It makes everything very difficult for them."

"Good heavens, I should think it did. What a darned silly principle. I mean to say, if one didn't do anything that wasn't worth doing well—why, what *would* one do? I've always maintained that success in this world depends on knowing exactly how little effort each job is worth . . . distribution of energy. . . . And, I suppose, most people would admit that I was a pretty successful man."

"Yes, I suppose they would, Outrage," said Father Rothschild, looking at him rather quizzically.

But that self-accusing voice in the Prime Minister's heart was silent. There was nothing like a little argument for settling the mind. Everything became so simple as soon as it was put into words.

"And anyway, what do you mean by 'historical'?"

"Well, it's like this war that's coming. . . ."

"What war?" said the Prime Minister sharply. "No one has said anything to me about a war. I really think I should have been told. I'll be damned," he said defiantly, "if they shall have a war without consulting me. What's a Cabinet for, if there's not more mutual

confidence than that? What do they want a war for, anyway?"

"That's the whole point. No one talks about it, and no one wants it. No one talks about it *because* no one wants it. They're all afraid to breathe a word about it."

"Well, hang it all, if no one wants it, who's going to make them have it?"

"Wars don't start nowadays because people want them. We long for peace, and fill our newspapers with conferences about disarmament and arbitration, but there is a radical instability in our whole world-order, and soon we shall all be walking into the jaws of destruction again, protesting our pacific intentions."

"Well, you seem to know all about it," said Mr. Outrage, "and I think I should have been told sooner. This will have to mean a coalition with that old windbag Brown, I suppose."

"Anyhow," said Lord Metroland, "I don't see how all that explains why my stepson should drink like a fish and go about everywhere with a negress."

"I think they're connected, you know," said Father Rothschild. "But it's all very difficult."

Then they separated.

Father Rothschild pulled on a pair of overall trousers in the forecourt, and, mounting his motor cycle, disappeared into the night, for he had many people to see and much business to transact before he went to bed.

Lord Metroland left the house in some depression. Margot had taken the car, but it was scarcely five minutes' walk to Hill Street. He took a vast cigar from his case, lit it and sank his chin in the astrakan collar of his coat, conforming almost exactly to the popular conception of a highly enviable man. But his heart was heavy. What a lot of nonsense Rothschild had talked. At least he hoped it was nonsense.

By ill-fortune he arrived on the doorstep to find Peter Pastmaster fumbling with the lock, and they entered together. Lord Metroland noticed a tall hat on the table by the door. "Young Trumpington's, I suppose," he thought. His stepson did not once look at him, but made straight for the stairs, walking unsteadily, his hat on the back of his head, his umbrella still in his hand.

"Good night, Peter," said Lord Metroland.

"Oh, go to hell," said his stepson thickly, then, turning on the stairs, he added, "I'm going abroad to-morrow for a few weeks. Will you tell my mother?"

"Have a good time," said Lord Metroland. "You'll

find it just as cold everywhere, I'm afraid. Would you care to take the yacht? No one's using it."

"Oh, go to hell."

Lord Metroland went into the study to finish his cigar. It would be awkward if he met young Trumpington on the stairs. He sat down in a very comfortable chair. . . . A radical instability, Rothschild had said, radical instability. . . . He looked round his study and saw shelves of books—the *Dictionary of National Biography*, the *Encyclopædia Britannica* in an early and very bulky edition, *Who's Who*, Debrett, Burke, Whitaker, several volumes of Hansard, some Blue Books and Atlases—a safe in the corner painted green with a brass handle, his writing-table, his secretary's table, some very comfortable chairs and some very businesslike chairs, a tray with decanters and a plate of sandwiches, his evening mail laid out on the table . . . radical instability, indeed. How like poor old Outrage to let himself get taken in by that charlatan of a Jesuit.

He heard the front door open and shut behind Alastair Trumpington.

Then he rose and went quietly upstairs, leaving his cigar smouldering in the ash-tray, filling the study with fragrant smoke.

187

Quarter of a mile away the Duchess of Stayle went, as she always did, to say good night to her eldest daughter. She crossed the room and drew up the window a few inches, for it was a cold and raw night. Then she went over to the bed and smoothed the pillow.

"Good night, dear child," she said. "I thought you looked sweet tonight."

Lady Ursula wore a white cambric night-gown with a little yoke collar and long sleeves. Her hair hung in two plaits.

"Mamma," she said. "Edward proposed to me tonight."

"*Darling*. What a funny girl you are. Why didn't you tell me before? You weren't frightened, were you? You know that your father and I are delighted at anything that makes our little girl happy."

"Well, I said I wouldn't marry him . . . I'm sorry."

"But, my dear, it's nothing to be sorry about. Leave it to your old mother. I'll put it all right for you in the morning."

"But, Mamma, I don't want to marry him. I didn't know until it actually came to the point. I'd always meant to marry him, as you know. But, somehow,

188

when he actually asked me . . . I just couldn't."

"There, dear child, you mustn't worry any more. You know perfectly well, don't you, that your father and I would not let you do anything you didn't want. It's a matter that only you can decide. After all, it's your life and your happiness at stake, not ours, isn't it, Ursula . . . but I *think* you'd better marry Edward."

"But, Mamma, I don't want to . . . I couldn't . . . it would kill me!"

"Now, now, my pet mustn't worry her head about it any more. You know your father and I only want *your* happiness, dear one. No one is going to make my darling girl do anything she doesn't want to. . . . Papa shall see Edward in the morning and make everything all right . . . dear Lady Anchorage was only saying tonight what a lovely bride you will make."

"But, Mamma . . ."

"Not another word, dear child. It's very late and you've got to look your best for Edward tomorrow, haven't you, love?"

The Duchess closed the door softly and went to her own room. Her husband was in his dressing-room.

"Andrew."

"What is it, dear? I'm saying my prayers."

"Edward proposed to Ursula tonight."

"Ah!"

"Aren't you glad?"

"I told you, dear, I'm trying to say my prayers."

"It's a real joy to see the dear children so happy."

IX

T luncheon time next day Adam rang up Nina.

"Nina, darling, are you awake?"

"Well, I wasn't . . ."

"Listen, do you really want me to go and see your papa today?"

"Did we say you were going to?"

"Yes."

"Why?"

"To say could we be married now I had a job."

"I remember . . . yes, go and see him, darling. It would be nice to be married."

"But, listen, what about my page?"

"What page, angel?"

"My page in the *Excess* . . . my job, you know."

"Oh . . . well, look . . . Ginger and I will write that for you."

"Wouldn't that be a bore?"

"I think it would be divine. I know just the sort of things you say. . . . I expect Ginger does too by now, the poor angel . . . how he did enjoy himself last night. . . . I'm going to sleep now . . . such a pain . . . good-bye, my sweet."

Adam had some luncheon. Agatha Runcible was at the next table with Archie Schwert. She said they were all going to some motor races next day. Would Adam and Nina come, too. Adam said yes. Then he went to Aylesbury.

There were two women on the other side of the carriage, and they, too, were talking about the Younger Generation.

". . . And it's a very good position, too, for a boy of that age, and I've told him and his father told him. 'You ought to think yourself lucky,' I've said, 'to get a good position like that in these days, particularly when it's so hard to get a position at all of any kind *or* sort.' And there's Mrs. Hemingway with her son next door who left school eighteen months ago, and there he is kicking his heels about the house all day and doing nothing, and taking a correspondence course in civil engineering. 'It's a very good position,' I told him, 'and, of course, you can't expect *work* to be interesting, though no doubt after a time you get used to it just as your father's done, and would probably miss it if you hadn't it to do,'—you know how Alfred gets on his holidays, doesn't know what to do with himself half the time, just looks at the sea and says, 'Well, this *is* a change,' and then starts wondering how things are at the office. Well, I told Bob that, but it's no good, and all he wants to do is to go into the motor business; well, as I said to him, the motor business is all right for them that have influence, but what could Bob hope to do throwing up a good job, too, and with nothing to fall back on supposing things did go wrong. But, no, Bob is all for motors, and, of course, you know it doesn't really do having him living at home. He and his father don't get on. You can't have two men in a house together and both wanting the bath at the same time, and I suppose it's only natural that Bob should feel he ought to have his own way a bit more now that he's earning his own money. But, then, what is he to do? He can't go and live on his own with his present salary, and I shouldn't be any too pleased to see him doing it even if he could afford it—you know what it is with young people, how easy it is to get into mischief when they're left to themselves. And there are

193

a great many of Bob's friends now that I don't really approve of, not to have in and out of the house, you know the way they do come. He meets them at the hockey club he goes to Saturdays. And they're most of them earning more money than he is, or, at any rate, they seem to have more to throw about, and it isn't good for a boy being about with those that have more money than him. It only makes him discontented. And I did think at one time that perhaps Bob was thinking of Betty Rylands, you know Mrs. Rylands' girl at the Laurels, such nice people, and they used to play tennis together and people remarked how much they were about, but now he never seems to pay any attention to her, it's all his hockey friends, and I said one Saturday, 'Wouldn't you like to ask Betty over to tea?' and he said, 'Well, you can if you like,' and she came looking ever so sweet, and, would you believe it, Bob went out and didn't come in at all until supper time. Well, you can't expect any girl to put up with that, and now she's practically engaged to that young Anderson boy who's in the wireless business."

"Well, and there's our Lily now. You know how she would go in for being a manicurist. Her father didn't like it, and for a long time he wouldn't have it at all. He said it was just an excuse for holding hands, but, anyway, I said, 'If that's what the girl wants to do, and if she can make good money doing it, I think you ought to be able to trust your own daughter better than to stand in her way.' I'm a modern, you see. 'We're not living in the Victorian Age,' I told him. Well, she's in a very nice job. Bond Street—and they treat her very fair, and we've no complaints on that score, but now there's this man she's met there—he's old enough to be her father—well, middle-aged anyway—but very smart, you know, neat little grey moustache, absolute gentleman, with a Morris Oxford saloon. And he comes and takes her out for drives Sundays, and sometimes he fetches her after work and takes her to the pictures, and always most polite and well spoken to me and my husband, just as you'd expect, seeing the sort of man he is, and he sent us all tickets for the theatre the other night. Very affable, calls me 'Ma,' if you please . . . and, anyway, I *hope* there's no harm in it . . ."

"Now our Bob . . ."

They got out at Berkhamsted, and a man got in who wore a bright brown suit and spent his time doing sums, which never seemed to come right, in a little

195

note-book with a stylographic pen. "Has he given all to his daughters?" thought Adam.

He drove out to Doubting by a bus which took him as far as the village of petrol pumps. From there he walked down the lane to the park gates. To his surprise these stood open, and as he approached he narrowly missed being run down by a large and ramshackle car which swept in at a high speed; he caught a glimpse of two malignant female eyes which glared contemptuously at him from the small window at the back. Still more surprising was a large notice which hung on the central pier of the gates and said: "No Admittance Except on Business." As Adam walked up the drive two lorries thundered past him. Then a man appeared with a red flag.

"Hi! You can't go that way. They're shooting in front. Go round by the stables, whoever you are."

Wondering vaguely what kind of sport this could be, Adam followed the side path indicated. He listened for sounds of firing, but hearing nothing except distant shouting and what seemed to be a string band, he concluded that the Colonel was having a poor day. It seemed odd, anyway, to go shooting in front of one's house with a string band, and automatically Adam began making up a paragraph about it:

"Colonel Blount, the father of the lovely Miss Nina Blount referred to above, rarely comes to London nowadays. He devotes himself instead to shooting on his estate in Buckinghamshire. The coverts, which are among the most richly stocked in the county, lie immediately in front of the house, and many amusing stories are related of visitors who have inadvertently found themselves in the line of fire. . . . Colonel Blount has the curious eccentricity of being unable to shoot his best except to the accompaniment of violin and 'cello. (Mr. 'Ginger' Littlejohn has the similar foible that he can only fish to the sound of the flageolet.) . . ."

He had not gone very far in his detour before he was again stopped, this time by a man dressed in a surplice, episcopal lawn sleeves and scarlet hood and gown; he was smoking a cigar.

"Here, what in hell do *you* want?" said the Bishop.

"I came to see Colonel Blount."

"Well, you can't, son. They're just shooting him now."

"Good heavens. What for?"

"Oh, nothing important. He's just one of the Wesleyans, you know—we're trying to polish off the whole crowd this afternoon while the weather's good."

Adam found himself speechless before this cold-blooded bigotry.

"What d'you want to see the old geyser about, anyway?"

"Well, it hardly seems any good now. I came to tell him that I'd got a job on the *Excess.*"

"The devil you have. Why didn't you say so before? Always pleased to see gentlemen of the Press. Have a weed?" A large cigar-case appeared from the recesses of the episcopal bosom. "I'm Bishop Philpotts, you know," he said, slipping a voluminously clothed arm through Adam's. "I dare say you'd like to come round to the front and see the fun. I should think they'd be just singing their last hymn now. It's been uphill work," he confided as they walked round the side of the house, "and there's been some damned bad management. Why, yesterday, they kept Miss La Touche waiting the whole afternoon, and then the light was so bad when they did shoot her that they made a complete mess of her—we had the machine out and ran over all the bits carefully last night after dinner—you never saw such rotten little scraps—quite unrecognizable, half of them. We didn't dare show them to her husband—he'd be sick to death about it—so we just cut out a few shots to keep and threw away

198

the rest. I say, you're not feeling queer, are you? You look all green suddenly. Find the weed a bit strong?"

"Was—was she a Wesleyan too?"

"My dear boy, she's playing lead . . . she's Selina, Countess of Huntingdon. . . . There, now you can see them at work."

They had rounded the wing and were now in full view of the front of the house, where all was activity and animation. A dozen or so men and women in eighteenth-century costume were standing in a circle singing strongly, while in their centre stood a small man in a long clerical coat and a full white wig, conducting them. A string band was playing not far off and round the singers clustered numerous men in shirt sleeves bearing megaphones, cinematograph cameras, microphones, sheaves of paper and arc lamps. Not far away, waiting their turn to be useful, stood a coach and four, a detachment of soldiers and some scene shifters with the transept of Exeter Cathedral in sections of canvas and match-boarding.

"The Colonel's somewhere in that little crowd singing the hymn," said the Bishop. "He was crazy to be allowed to come on as a super, and as he's letting us the house dirt cheap Isaacs said he might. I don't believe he's ever been so happy in his life."

199

As they approached, the hymn stopped.

"All right," said one of the men with megaphones. "You can beat it. We'll shoot the duel now. I shall want two supers to carry the body. The rest of you are through for the afternoon."

A man in a leather apron, worsted stockings and flaxen wig emerged from the retreating worshippers.

"Oh, please, Mr. Isaacs," he said, "please may *I* carry the body?"

"All right, Colonel, if you want to. Run in and tell them in the wardrobe to give you a smock and a pitchfork."

"Thank you so much," said Colonel Blount, trotting off towards his house. Then he stopped. "I suppose," he said, "I suppose it wouldn't be better for me to carry a sword?"

"No, pitchfork, and hurry up about it or I shan't let you carry the body at all; someone go and find Miss La Touche."

The young lady whom Adam had seen in the motor car came down the steps of the house in a feathered hat, riding habit and braided cape. She carried a hunting crop in her hand. Her face was painted very yellow.

"Do I or do I not have a horse in this scene, Mr.

200

Isaacs? I've been round to Bertie and he says all the horses are needed for the coach."

"I'm sorry. Effie, you do *not* and it's no good taking on. We only got four horses and you know that, and you saw what it was like when we tried to move the coach with two. So you've just got to face it. You comes across the fields on foot."

"Dirty Yid.," said Effie La Touche.

"The trouble about this film," said the Bishop, "is that we haven't enough capital. It's heart-breaking. Here we have a first-rate company, first-rate producer, first-rate scene, first-rate story and the whole thing being hung up for want of a few hundred pounds. How can he expect to get the best out of Miss La Touche if they won't give her a horse? No girl will stand for that sort of treatment. If I were Isaacs I'd scrap the whole coach sooner. It's no sense getting a star and not treating her right. Isaacs is putting everyone's back up the way he goes on. Wanted to do the whole of my cathedral scene with twenty-five supers. But you're here to give us a write-up, aren't you? I'll call Isaacs across and let him give you the dope. . . . *Isaacs!*"

"Yuh?"

"*Daily Excess* here."

"Where?"

"Here."

"I'll be right over." He put on his coat, buttoned it tightly at the waist and strode across the lawn, extending a hand of welcome. Adam shook it and felt what seemed to be a handful of rings under his fingers. "Pleased to meet you, Mister. Now just you ask me anything you want about this film because I'm just here to answer. Have you got my name? Have a card. That's the name of the company in the corner. Not the one that's scratched out. The one written above. *The Wonderfilm Company of Great Britain.* Now this film," he said, in what seemed a well-practised little speech, "of which you have just witnessed a mere fragment, marks a stepping stone in the development of the British Film Industry. It is the most important All-Talkie super-religious film to be produced solely in this country by British artists and management and by British capital. It has been directed throughout regardless of difficulty and expense, and supervised by a staff of expert historians and theologians. Nothing has been omitted that would contribute to the meticulous accuracy of every detail. The life of that great social and religious reformer John Wesley is for the first time portrayed to a British public in all its humanity

202

and tragedy. . . . Look here, I've got all this written out. I'll have them give you a copy before you go. Come and see the duel. . . .

"That's Wesley and Whitefield just going to start. Of course, it's not them really. Two fencing instructors we got over from the gym at Aylesbury. That's what I mean when I say we spare no expense to get the details accurate. Ten bob each we're paying them for the afternoon."

"But did Wesley and Whitefield fight a duel?"

"Well, it's not actually recorded, but it's known that they quarrelled and there was only one way of settling quarrels in those days. They're both in love with Selina, Countess of Huntingdon, you see. She comes to stop them, but arrives too late. Whitefield has escaped in the coach and Wesley is lying wounded. That's a scene that'll go over big. Then she takes him back to her home and nurses him back to health. I tell you, this is going to make film history. D'you know what the Wesleyan population of the British Isles is? Well, nor do I, but I've been told and *you'd be surprised*. Well, every one of those is going to come and see this film and there's going to be discussions about it in all the chapels. We're recording extracts from Wesley's sermons and we're singing all his own

203

hymns. I'm glad your paper's interested. You can tell them from me that we're on a big thing. . . . There's one thing though," said Mr. Isaacs, suddenly becoming confidential, "which I shouldn't tell many people. But I think you'll understand because you've seen some of our work here and the sort of scale it's on, and you can imagine that expenses are pretty heavy. Why, I'm paying Miss La Touche alone over ten pounds a week. And the truth is—I don't mind telling you—we're beginning to feel the wind a bit. It's going to be a big success *when* and *if* it's finished. Now, suppose there was someone—yourself, for instance, or one of your friends—who had a little bit of loose capital he wanted to invest—a thousand pounds, say —well, I wouldn't mind selling him a half share. It's not a gamble, mind—it's a certain winner. If I cared to go into the open market with it, it would be snapped up before you could say knife. But I don't want to do that and I'll tell you why. This is a British Company and I don't want to let any of those foreign speculators in on it, and once you let the shares get into the open market you can't tell who's buying them, see. Now why leave money idle bringing in four and a half or five per cent. when you might be doubling it in six months?"

204

"I'm afraid it's no use coming to me for capital," said Adam. "Do you think I could possibly see Colonel Blount?"

"One of the things I hate in life," said Mr. Isaacs, "is seeing anyone lose an opportunity. Now listen, I'll make you a fair offer. I can see you're interested in this film. Now I'll sell you the whole thing—film we've made up to date, artists' contracts, copyright of scenario, everything for five hundred quid. Then all you have to do is to finish it off and your fortune's made and I shall be cursing for not having held on longer. How about it?"

"It's very good of you, but really I don't think I can afford it at the moment."

"Just as you like," said Mr. Isaacs airily. "There's many who *can* who'd jump at the offer, only I thought I'd let you in on it first because I could see you were a smart kid. . . . Tell you what I'll do. I'll let you have it for four hundred. Can't say fairer than that, can I? And wouldn't do it for anyone but you."

"I'm terribly sorry, Mr. Isaacs, but I didn't come to buy your film. I came to see Colonel Blount."

"Well, I shouldn't have thought you were the sort of chap to let an opportunity like that slip through your fingers. Now I'll give you one more chance and

205

after that, mind, the offer is closed. I'll sell you it for three-fifty. Take it or leave it. That's my last word. Of course, you're not in any way obliged to buy," said Mr. Isaacs rather haughtily, "but I assure you that you'll regret it from the bottom of your heart if you don't."

"I'm sorry," said Adam, "I think it's a wonderfully generous offer, but the truth is I simply don't want to buy a film at all."

"In that case," said Mr. Isaacs, "I shall return to my business."

Not until sunset did the Wonderfilm Company of Great Britain rest. Adam watched them from the lawn. He saw the two fencing instructors in long black coats and white neck bands lunging and parrying manfully until one of them fell; then the cameras stopped and his place was taken by the leading actor (who had been obliged through the exigencies of the wardrobe to lend his own coat). Whitefield took the place (and the wig) of the victor and fled to the coach. Effie La 'Touche appeared from the shrubbery still defiantly carrying her hunting crop. Close-ups followed of Effie and Wesley and Effie and Wesley together. Then Colonel Blount and another super appeared as yokels and carried the wounded preacher

206

back to the house. All this took a long time as the action was frequently held up by minor mishaps and once when the whole scene had been triumphantly enacted the chief cameraman found that he had forgotten to put in a new roll of film ("Can't think how I come to make a mistake like that, Mr. Isaacs"). Finally the horses were taken out of the coach and mounted by grenadiers and a few shots taken of them plunging despairingly up the main drive.

"Part of Butcher Cumberland's army," explained Mr. Isaacs. "It's always good to work in a little atmosphere like that. Gives more educational value. Besides we hire the horses by the day so we might as well get all we can out of them while they're here. If we don't use 'em in Wesley we can fit 'em in somewhere else. A hundred foot or so of galloping horses is always useful."

When everything was over, Adam managed to see Colonel Blount, but it was not a satisfactory interview.

"I'm afraid I've really got very little time to spare," he said. "To tell you the truth, I'm at work on a scenario of my own. They tell me you come from the *Excess* and want to write about the film. It's a glorious film, isn't it? Of course, you know, I have very

207

little to do with it really. I have let them the house
and have acted one or two small parts in the crowd. I
don't have to pay for them though."

"No, I should think not."

"My dear boy, all the others have to. I knocked a
little off the rent of the house, but I don't actually
pay. In fact, you might almost say I was a professional already. You see, Mr. Isaacs is the principal of
the National Academy of Cinematographic Art. He's
got a little office in Edgware Road, just one room, you
know, to interview candidates in. Well, if he thinks
that they're promising enough—he doesn't take anyone, mind, only a chosen few—he takes them on as
pupils. As Mr. Isaacs says, the best kind of training is
practical work, so he produces a film straight away and
pays the professionals out of the pupils' fees. It's really
a very simple and sensible plan. All the characters in
'John Wesley' are pupils, except Wesley himself and
Whitefield and the Bishop and, of course, Miss La
Touche—she's the wife of the man who looks after
the Edgware Road office when Mr. Isaacs is away.
Even the cameramen are only learning. It makes
everything so exciting, you know. This is the third
film Mr. Isaacs has produced. The first went wrong,
through Mr. Isaacs trusting one of the pupils to de-
208

velop it. Of course, he made him pay damages—that's in the contract they all have to sign—but the film was ruined, and Mr. Isaacs said it was disheartening—he nearly gave up the cinema altogether. But then a lot more pupils came along, so they produced another, which was *very* good indeed. Quite a revolution in Film Art, Mr. Isaacs said, but that was boycotted through professional jealousy. None of the theatres would show it. But that's been made all right now. Mr. Isaacs has got in with the ring, he says, and this is going to establish Wonderfilms as the leading company in the country. What's more, he's offered me a half share in it for five thousand pounds. It's wonderfully generous, when he might keep it all to himself, but he says that he must have someone who understands *acting* from the practical side on the board of directors. Funnily enough, my bank manager is very much against my going in for it. In fact, he's putting every obstacle in my way. . . . But I dare say Mr. Isaacs would sooner you didn't put any of this into your paper."

"What I really came about was your daughter, Nina."

"Oh, she's not taking any part in the film at all. To tell you the truth, I very much doubt whether she has

209

any real talent. It's funny how these things often skip a generation. My father, now, was a very bad actor indeed—though he always used to take a leading part when we had theatricals at Christmas. Upon my soul, he used to make himself look quite ridiculous sometimes. I remember once he did a skit of Henry Irving in 'The Bells.' . . ."

"I'm afraid you've forgotten me, sir, but I came here last month to see you about Nina. Well, she wanted me to tell you that I'm Mr. Chatterbox now. . . ."

"Chatterbox . . . no, my boy, I'm afraid I don't remember you. My memory's not what it was. . . . There's a Canon Chatterbox at Worcester I used to know . . . he was up at New College with me . . . unusual name."

"Mr. Chatterbox on the *Daily Excess*."

"No, no, my dear boy, I assure you not. He was ordained just after I went down and was chaplain somewhere abroad—Bermuda, I think. Then he came home and went to Worcester. He was never on the *Daily Excess* in his life."

"No, no, sir, *I'm* on the *Daily Excess*."

"Well, you ought to know your own staff, certainly.

He *may* have left Worcester and taken to journalism. A great many parsons do nowadays, I know. But I must say that he's the last fellow I should have expected it of. Awful stupid fellow. Besides, he must be at least seventy. . . . Well, well . . . who would have thought it. Good-bye, my boy, I've enjoyed our talk."

"Oh, sir," cried Adam, as Colonel Blount began to walk away. "You don't understand—I want to marry Nina."

"Well, it's no good coming here," said the Colonel crossly. "I told you, she's somewhere in London. She's got nothing to do with the film at all. You'll have to go and ask her about it. Anyway, I happen to know she's engaged already. There was a young ass of a chap down here about it the other day . . . the Rector said he was off his head. Laughed the whole time —bad sign that—still, Nina wants to marry him for some reason. So I'm afraid you're too late, my boy. I'm sorry . . . and, anyway, the Rector's behaved very badly about this film. Wouldn't lend his car. I suppose it's because of the Wesleyanism. Narrowminded, that. . . . Well, good-bye. So nice of you to come. Remember me to Canon Chatterbox. I must look him up next time I come to London and pull his leg about it. . . . Writing for the papers, indeed, at his age."

And Colonel Blount retired victorious.

Late that evening Adam and Nina sat in the gallery of the Café de la Paix eating oysters.

"Well we won't bother any more about papa," she said. "We'll just get married at once."

"We shall be terribly poor."

"Well, we shan't be any poorer than we are now. . . . I think it will be divine. . . . Besides, we'll be terribly economical. Miles says he's discovered a place near Tottenham Court Road where you can get oysters for three and six a dozen."

"Wouldn't they be rather ill-making?"

"Well, Miles said the only odd thing about them is that they all taste a little different. . . . I had lunch with Miles today. He rang up to find where you were. He wanted to sell Edward Throbbing's engagement to the *Excess*. But Van offered him five guineas for it, so he gave it to them."

"I'm sorry we missed that. The editor will be furious. By the way, how did the gossip page go? Did you manage to fill it all right?"

"My dear, I think I did rather well. You see Van and Miles didn't know I was in the trade, so they talked about Edward's engagement a whole lot, so I went and put it in . . . was that very caddish? . . . and I wrote a lot about Edward and the girl he's to marry. I used to know her when I came out, and that took up half the page. So I just put in a few imaginary ones like you do, so then it was finished."

"What did you say in the imaginary ones?"

"Oh, I don't know. I said I saw Count Cincinnati going into Espinosa's in a green bowler . . . things like that."

"*You said that?*"

"Yes, wasn't it a good thing to say. . . . Angel, is anything wrong?"

"Oh, God."

Adam dashed to the telephone.

"Central ten thousand . . . put me through to the night editor. . . . Look here, I've got to make a correction in the Chatterbox page . . . it's urgent."

"Sorry, Symes. Last edition went to bed half an hour ago. Got everything made up early tonight."

So Adam went back to finish his oysters.

"Bad tabulation there," said Lord Monomark next morning, when he saw the paragraph.

So Miles Malpractice became Mr. Chatterbox.

"Now we can't be married," said Nina.

X

 DAM and Miss Runcible and Miles and Archie Schwert went up to the motor races in Archie Schwert's car. It was a long and cold drive. Miss Runcible wore trousers and Miles touched up his eyelashes in the dining-room of the hotel where they stopped for luncheon. So they were asked to leave. At the next hotel they made Miss Runcible stay outside, and brought her cold lamb and pickles in the car. Archie thought it would be nice to have champagne, and worried the wine waiter about dates (a subject which had always been repugnant to him). They spent a long time over luncheon because it was warm there, and they drank Kümmel over the fire until Miss Runcible came in very angrily to fetch them out.

Then Archie said he was too sleepy to drive any more, so Adam changed places with him and lost the

215

way, and they travelled miles in the wrong direction down a limitless bye-pass road.

And then it began to be dark and the rain got worse. They stopped for dinner at another hotel, where every one giggled at Miss Runcible's trousers in a dining-room hung with copper warming pans.

Presently they came to the town where the race was to be run. They drove to the hotel where the dirt-track racer was staying. It was built in the Gothic style of 1860, large, dark and called the Imperial.

They had wired him to book them rooms, but "Bless you," said the woman at the counter marked "Reception," "all our rooms have been booked for the last six months. I couldn't fit you in anywhere, not if you was the Speed Kings themselves, I couldn't. I don't suppose you'll find anything in the town tonight. You might try at the Station Hotel. That's your only chance."

At the Station Hotel they made Miss Runcible wait outside, but with no better success.

"I might put one of you on the sofa in the bar parlour, there's only a married couple in there at present and two little boys, or if you didn't mind sit-ting up all night, there's always the palm lounge." As for a bed, that was out of the question. They might

216

try at the "Royal George," but she doubted very much whether they'd *like* that even if there was room, which she was pretty sure there was not."

Then Miss Runcible thought that she remembered that there were some friends of her father who lived quite near, so she found out their telephone number and rang them up, but they said no, they were sorry, but they had a completely full house and practically no servants, and that as far as they knew they had never heard of Lord Chasm. So that was no good.

Then they went to several more hotels, sinking through the various gradations of Old Established Family and Commercial, plain Commercial, High Class Board Residence pension terms, Working Girls' Hostel, plain Pub. and Clean Beds: Gentlemen only. All were full. At last, by the edge of a canal they came to the "Royal George." The landlady stood at the door and rounded off an argument with an elderly little man in a bowler hat.

"First 'e takes off 'is boots in the saloon bar," she said, enlisting the sympathy of her new audience, "which is not the action of a gentleman."

"They was wet," said the little man; "wet as 'ell."

"Well, and who wants your wet boots on the counter, I should like to know. Then, if you please, he calls

217

me a conspiring woman because I tells him to stop and put them on before he goes 'ome."

"Want to go 'ome," said the little man. " 'Ome to my wife and kids. *Trying to keep a man from 'is wife.*"

"No one wants to keep you from your wife, you old silly. All I says is for Gawd's sake put on your boots before you go 'ome. What'll your wife think of you coming 'ome without boots."

"She won't mind 'ow I come 'ome. Why, bless you, I ain't been 'ome at all for five years. It's 'ard to be separated from a wife and kids by a conspiring woman trying to make yer put on yer boots."

"My dear, she's quite right, you know," said Miss Runcible. "You'd far better put on your boots."

"There, 'ear what the lady says. Lady says you've to put on your boots."

The little man took his boots from the landlady, looked at Miss Runcible with a searching glance, and threw them into the canal. *"Lady,"* he said with feeling. *"Trousers,"* and then he paddled off in his socks into the darkness.

"There ain't no 'arm in 'im really," said the landlady, "only he do get a bit wild when he's 'ad the drink. Wasting good boots like that. . . . I expect he'll spend the night in the lock-up."

218

"Won't he get back to his wife, poor sweet?"

"Lor' bless you, no. She lives in London."

At this stage Archie Schwert, whose humanitarian interests were narrower than Miss Runcible's, lost interest in the discussion.

"The thing we want to know is, can you let us have beds for the night?"

The landlady looked at him suspiciously.

"Bed or beds?"

"Beds."

"Might do." She looked from the car to Miss Runcible's trousers and back to the car again, weighing them against each other. "Cost you a quid each," she said at last.

"Can you find room for us all?"

"Well," she said, "which of you's with the young lady?"

"I'm afraid I'm all alone," said Miss Runcible. "Isn't it too shaming?"

"Never you mind, dearie, luck'll turn one day. Well, now, how can we all fit in? There's one room empty. I can sleep with our Sarah, and that leaves a bed for the gentlemen—then if the young lady wouldn't mind coming in with me and Sarah . . ."

"If you don't think it rude, I think I'd sooner have

the empty bed," said Miss Runcible, rather faintly. "You see," she added, with tact, "I snore so terribly."

"Bless you, so does our Sarah. *We* don't mind . . . still, if you'd *rather* . . ."

"Really, I think I should," said Miss Runcible.

"Well then, I could put Mr. Titchcock on the floor, couldn't I?"

"Yes," said Miles, "just you put Mr. Titchcock on the floor."

"And if the other gentleman don't mind going on the landing. . . . Well, we'll manage somehow, see if we don't."

So they all drank some gin together in the back parlour and they woke Mr. Titchcock up and made him help with the luggage and they gave him some gin, too, and he said it was all the same to him whether he slept on the floor or in bed, and he was very pleased to be of any service to anyone and didn't mind if he did have another drop just as a night-cap, as they might say; and at last they all went to bed, very tired, but fairly contented, and oh, how they were bitten by bugs all that night.

Adam had secured one of the bedrooms. He awoke early to find rain beating on the window. He looked out and saw a grey sky, some kind of factory and the canal from whose shallow waters rose little islands of scrap-iron and bottles; a derelict perambulator lay partially submerged under the opposite bank. In his room stood a chest of drawers full of horrible fragments of stuff, a wash-hand stand with a highly coloured basin, an empty jug and an old toothbrush. There was also a rotund female bust covered in shiny red material, and chopped off short, as in primitive martyrdoms, at neck, waist and elbows; a thing known as a dressmaker's "dummy" (there had been one of these in Adam's home which they used to call "Jemima"—one day he stabbed "Jemima" with a chisel and scattered stuffing over the nursery floor and was punished. A more enlightened age would have seen a complex in this action and worried accordingly. Anyway he was made to sweep up all the stuffing himself).

Adam was very thirsty, but there was a light green moss in the bottom of the water bottle that repelled him. He got into bed again and found someone's handkerchief (presumably Mr. Titchcock's) under the pillow.

He woke again a little later to find Miss Runcible, dressed in pyjamas and a fur coat, sitting on his bed.

"Darling," she said, "there's no looking-glass in my

221

room and no bath anywhere, and I trod on someone cold and soft asleep in the passage, and I've been awake all night killing bugs with drops of face lotion, and everything smells, and I feel so low I could die."

"For heaven's sake let's go away," said Adam.

So they woke Miles and Archie Schwert, and ten minutes later they all stole out of the "Royal George" carrying their suitcases.

"I wonder, do you think we ought to leave some money?" asked Adam, but the others all said no.

"Well, perhaps we ought to pay for the gin," said Miss Runcible.

So they left five shillings on the bar and drove away to the "Imperial."

It was still very early, but everyone seemed to be awake, running in and out of the lifts carrying crash helmets and overalls. Miles' friend, they were told, had been out before dawn, presumably at his garage. Adam met some reporters whom he used to see about the *Excess* office. They told him that it was anyone's race, and that the place to see the fun was Headlong Corner, where there had been three deaths the year before, and it was worse this year, because they'd been putting down wet tar. It was nothing more or

222

less than a death trap, the reporters said. Then they went away to interview some more drivers. All teams were confident of victory, they said.

Meanwhile Miss Runcible discovered an empty bathroom, and came down half an hour later all painted up and wearing a skirt and feeling quite herself again and ready for anything. So they went in to breakfast.

The dining-room was very full indeed. There were Speed Kings of all nationalities, unimposing men mostly with small moustaches and apprehensive eyes; they were reading the forecasts in the morning papers and eating what might (and in some cases did) prove to be their last meal on earth. There were a great number of journalists making the best of an "out-of-town" job; there were a troop of nondescript "fans," knowledgeable young men with bright jumpers tucked inside their belted trousers, old public-school ties, check tweeds, loose mouths and scarcely discernible Cockney accents; there were R.A.C. officials and A.A. officials, and the representatives of oil firms and tyre manufacturers. There was one disconsolate family who had come to the town for the christening of a niece. (No one had warned them that there was a motor race on; their hotel bill *was* a shock.)

223

"Very better-making," said Miss Runcible with approval as she ate her haddock.

Scraps of highly technical conversation rose on all sides of them.

". . . Changed the whole engine over after they'd been scrutineered. Anyone else would have been disqualified . . ."

". . . Just cruising round at fifty . . ."

". . . Stung by a bee just as he was taking the corner, missed the tree by inches and landed up in the Town Hall. There was a Riley coming up behind, spun round twice, climbed the bank, turned right over and caught fire . . ."

". . . Local overheating at the valve-heads. It's no sense putting a supercharger in that engine at all . . ."

". . . Headlong Corner's jam. All you want to do is to break right down to forty or forty-five at the white cottage, then rev. up opposite the pub. and get straight away in second on the near side of the road. A child could do it. It's that double bend just after the railway bridge where you'll get the funny stuff."

". . . Kept flagging him down from the pits. I tell you that bunch don't want him to win."

". . . She wouldn't tell me her name, but she said she'd meet me at the same place tonight and gave me

224

a sprig of white heather for the car. I lost it, like a fool. She said she'd look out for it too . . ."

". . . Only offers a twenty pound bonus this year . . ."

". . . Lapped at seventy-five . . ."

". . . Burst his gasket and blew out his cylinder heads . . ."

". . . Broke both arms and cracked his skull in two places . . ."

". . . Tailwag . . ."

". . . Speed-wobble . . ."

". . . Merc . . ."

". . . Mag . . ."

". . . Crash . . ."

When they finished breakfast, Miss Runcible and Adam and Archie Schwert and Miles went to the garage to look for their Speed King. They found him hard at work listening to his engine. A corner of the garage had been roped off and the floor strewn with sand as though for a boxing match.

Outside this ring clustered a group of predatory little boys with autograph albums and leaking fountain pens, and inside, surrounded by attendants, stood the essential parts of a motor car. The engine was running and the whole machine shook with fruitless exertion.

Clouds of dark smoke came from it, and a shattering roar which reverberated from concrete floor and corrugated iron roof into every corner of the building so that speech and thought became insupportable and all the senses were numbed. At frequent intervals this high and heart-breaking note was varied by sharp detonations, and it was these apparently which were causing anxiety, for at each report Miles' friend, who clearly could not have been unduly sensitive to noise, gave a little wince and looked significantly at his head mechanic.

Apart from the obvious imperfection of its sound, the car gave the impression to an uninstructed observer of being singularly unfinished. In fact, it was obviously still under construction. It had only three wheels; the fourth being in the hands of a young man in overalls, who, in the intervals of tossing back from his eyes a curtain of yellow hair, was beating it with a hammer. It also had no seats, and another mechanic was screwing down slabs of lead ballast in the place where one would have expected to find them. It had no bonnet; that was in the hands of a sign painter, who was drawing a black number 13 in a white circle. There was a similar number on the back, and a mechanic was engaged in fixing another number board

226

over one of the headlights. There was a mechanic, too, making a windscreen of wire gauze, and a mechanic lying flat doing something to the back axle with a tin of grate polish and a rag. Two more mechanics were helping Miles' friend to listen to the bangs. "As if we couldn't have heard them from Berkeley Square," said Miss Runcible.

The truth is, that motor cars offer a very happy illustration of the metaphysical distinction between "being" and "becoming." Some cars, mere vehicles with no purpose above bare locomotion, mechanical drudges such as Lady Metroland's Hispano-Suiza, or Mrs. Mouse's Rolls Royce, or Lady Circumference's 1912 Daimler, or the "general reader's" Austin Seven, these have definite "being" just as much as their occupants. They are bought all screwed up and numbered and painted, and there they stay through various declensions of ownership, brightened now and then with a lick of paint or temporarily rejuvenated by the addition of some minor organ, but still maintaining their essential identity to the scrap heap.

Not so the *real* cars, that become masters of men; those vital creations of metal who exist solely for their own propulsion through space, for whom their drivers, clinging precariously at the steering wheel, are as

227

important as his stenographer to a stock-broker. These are in perpetual flux; a vortex of combining and disintegrating units; like the confluence of traffic at some spot where many roads meet, streams of mechanism come together, mingle and separate again.

Miles' friend, even had it been possible in the uproar, seemed indisposed to talk. He waved abstractedly and went on with his listening. Presently he came across and shouted:

"Sorry I can't spare a moment, I'll see you in the pits. I've got you some brassards."

"My dear, what *can* that be?"

He handed them each a strip of white linen, terminating in tape.

"For your arms," he shouted. "You can't get into the pits without them."

"My dear, what bliss! Fancy them having pits."

Then they tied on their brassards. Miss Runcible's said, "SPARE DRIVER"; Adam's, "DEPOT STAFF"; Miles', "SPARE MECHANIC"; and Archie's "OWNER'S REPRESENTATIVE."

Up till now the little boys round the rope had been sceptical of the importance of Miss Runcible and her friends, but as soon as they saw these badges of rank

228

they pressed forward with their autograph books. Archie signed them all with the utmost complaisance, and even drew a slightly unsuitable picture in one of them. Then they drove away in Archie's car.

The race was not due to start until noon, but any indecision which they may have felt about the employment of the next few hours was settled for them by the local police, who were engaged in directing all traffic, irrespective of its particular inclinations, on the road to the course. No pains had been spared about this point of organization; several days before, the Chief Constable had issued a little route map which was to be memorized by all constables on point duty, and so well had they learned their lesson that from early that morning until late in the afternoon no vehicle approaching the town from any direction escaped being drawn into that broad circuit marked by the arrows and dotted line A–B which led to the temporary car park behind the Grand Stand (Many doctors, thus diverted, spent an enjoyable day without apparent prejudice to their patients.)

The advance of the spectators had already assumed the form of a slow and unbroken stream. Some came on foot from the railway station, carrying sandwiches and camp stools; some on tandem bicycles; some in "runabouts" or motor cycle side-car combinations, but most were in modestly priced motor cars. Their clothes and demeanour proclaimed them as belonging to the middle rank; a few brought portable wireless sets with them and other evidence of gaiety, but the general air of the procession was one of sobriety and purpose. This was no Derby day holiday-making; they had not snatched a day from office to squander it among gipsies and roundabouts and thimble-and-pea men. They were there for the race. As they crawled along on bottom gear in a fog of exhaust gas, they discussed the technicalities of motor-car design and the possibilities of bloodshed, and studied their maps of the course to pick out the most dangerous corners.

The detour planned by the Chief Constable was a long one, lined with bungalows and converted railway carriages. Banners floated over it between the telegraph posts, mostly advertising the *London Despatch,* which was organizing the race and paying for the victor's trophy—a silver gilt figure of odious design, symbolizing Fame embracing Speed. (This at the moment was under careful guard in the stewards' room, for the year before it had been stolen on the eve of the race by the official time-keeper, who pawned it for a ridiculously small sum in Manchester, and was subsequently deprived of his position and sent to jail.) Other advertisements proclaimed the superiorities of various sorts of petrol and sparking plugs, while some said "£100 FOR LOSS OF LIMB. INSURE TODAY." There was an elderly man walking among the motor cars with a blue and white banner inscribed, "WITHOUT SHEDDING OF BLOOD IS NO REMISSION OF SIN," while a smartly dressed young man was doing a brisk trade in bogus tickets for the Grand Stand.

Adam sat in the back of the car with Miles, who was clearly put out about his friend's lack of cordiality. "What I can't make out," he said, "is why we came to this beastly place at all. I suppose I ought to be thinking of something to write for the *Excess*. I *know* this is just going to be the most dreary day we've ever spent."

Adam felt inclined to agree. Suddenly he became aware that someone was trying to attract his attention.

"There's an awful man shouting 'Hi' at you," said Miles. "My dear, *your friends.*"

Adam turned and saw not three yards away, separated from him by a young woman riding a push-bicycle in khaki shorts, her companion, who bore a knapsack on his shoulders, and a small boy selling programs, the long-sought figure of the drunk Major. He looked sober enough this morning, dressed in a bowler hat and Burberry, and he was waving frantically to Adam from the dicky of a coupé car.

"Hi!" cried the drunk Major. "Hi! I've been looking for you everywhere."

"I've been looking for you," shouted Adam. "I want some money."

"Can't hear—what do you want?"

"Money."

"It's no good—these infernal things make too much noise. What's your name? Lottie had forgotten."

"Adam Symes."

"Can't hear."

The line of traffic, creeping forward yard by yard, had at last reached the point B on the Chief Constable's map, where the dotted lines diverged. A policeman stood at the crossing directing the cars right and left, some to the parking place behind the Grand Stand, others to the mound above the pits. Archie turned off to the left. The drunk Major's car accellerated and swept away to the right.

"*I must know your name,*" he cried. All the drivers seemed to choose this moment to sound their
232

horns; the woman cyclist at Adam's elbow rang her bell; the male cylist tooted a little horn like a Paris taxi, and the program boy yelled in his ear, "Official program—map of the course—all the drivers."

"Adam Symes," he shouted desperately, but the Major threw up his hands in despair and he disappeared in the crowd.

"The way you pick people up . . ." said Miles, startled into admiration.

"The pits" turned out to be a line of booths, built of wood and corrugated iron immediately opposite the Grand Stand. Many of the cars had already arrived and stood at their "pits," surrounded by a knot of mechanics and spectators; they seemed to be already under repair. Busy officials hurried up and down, making entries in their lists. Over their heads a vast loud-speaker was relaying the music of a military band.

The Grand Stand was still fairly empty, but the rest of the course was already lined with people. It stretched up and down hill for a circle of thirteen or fourteen miles, and those who were fortunate enough to own cottages or public houses at the more dangerous corners had covered their roofs with unstable wooden forms, and were selling tickets like very ex-

233

pensive hot cakes. A grass-covered hill rose up sharply behind the pits. On this had been erected a hoarding where a troop of Boy Scouts were preparing to score the laps, passing the time contentedly with ginger beer, toffee, and rough-and-tumble fights. Behind the hoarding was a barbed-wire fence, and behind that again a crowd of spectators and several refreshment tents. A wooden bridge, advertising the *London Despatch*, had been built on the road. At various points officials might be seen attempting to understand each other over a field telephone. Sometimes the band would stop and a voice would announce, "Will Mr. So-and-So kindly report at once to the time-keeper's office"; then the band would go on.

Miss Runcible and her party found their way to the pit numbered 13 and sat on the match-board counter smoking and signing autograph books. An official bore down on them.

"No smoking in the pits, please."

"My dear, I'm terribly sorry. I didn't know."

There were six open churns behind Miss Runcible, four containing petrol and two water. She threw her cigarette over her shoulder, and by a beneficent attention of Providence, which was quite rare in her career, it fell into the water. Had it fallen into the

234

petrol it would probably have been all up with Miss Runcible.

Presently No. 13 appeared. Miles' friend and his mechanic wearing overalls, crash helmets, and goggles, jumped out, opened the bonnet and began to reconstruct it again.

"They didn't ought to have a No. 13 at all," said the mechanic. "It isn't fair."

Miss Runcible lit another cigarette.

"No smoking in the pits, *please*," said the official.

"My dear, how *awful* of me. I quite forgot."

(This time it fell in the mechanic's luncheon basket and lay smouldering quietly on a leg of chicken until it had burnt itself out.)

Miles' friend began filling up his petrol tank with the help of a very large funnel.

"Listen," he said. "You're not allowed to hand me anything direct, but if Edwards holds up his left hand as we come past the pits, that means we shall be stopping next lap for petrol. So what you've got to do is to fill up a couple of cans and put them on the shelf with the funnel for Edwards to take. If Edwards holds up his right hand . . ." elaborate instructions followed. "You're in charge of the depot," he said to Archie. "D'you think you've got all the signals clear?

The race may depend on them, remember."

"What does it mean if I wave the blue flag?"

"That you want me to stop."

"Why should I want you to stop?"

"Well, you might see something wrong—leaking tank or anything like that, or the officials might want the number plate cleaned."

"I think perhaps I won't do anything much about the blue flag. It seems rather too bogus for me."

Miss Runcible lit another cigarette.

"Will you kindly leave the pits if you wish to smoke?" said the official.

"What a damned rude man," said Miss Runcible. "Let's go up to that divine tent and get a drink."

They climbed the hill past the Boy Scouts, found a gate in the wire fence, and eventually reached the refreshment tent. Here an atmosphere of greater geniality prevailed. A profusion of men in plus-fours were having "quick ones" before the start. There was no nonsense about not smoking. There was a middle-aged woman sitting on the grass with a bottle of stout and a baby.

"Home from home," said Miss Runcible.

Suddenly the military band stopped and a voice

said, "Five minutes to twelve. All drivers and mechanics on the other side of the track, please."

There was a hush all over the course, and the refreshment tent began to empty quickly.

"Darling, we shall miss the start."

"Still, a drink *would* be nice."

So they went into the tent.

"Four whiskies, please," said Archie Schwert.

"You'll miss the start," said the barmaid.

"What a pig that man was," said Miss Runcible. "Even if we weren't supposed to smoke, he might at least have asked us politely."

"My dear, it was only you."

"Well, I think that made it worse."

"Lor', Miss," said the barmaid. "You surely ain't going to miss the start?"

"It's the one thing I want to see more than anything . . . my dear, I believe they're off already."

The sudden roar of sixty high-power engines rose from below. "They *have* started . . . how too shaming." They went to the door of the tent. Part of the road was visible over the heads of the spectators, and they caught a glimpse of the cars running all jammed together like pigs being driven through a gate; one by

237

one they shook themselves free and disappeared round the bend with a high shriek of acceleration.

"They'll be round again in quarter of an hour," said Archie. "Let's have another drink."

"Who was ahead?" asked the barmaid anxiously.

"I couldn't see for certain," said Miss Runcible, "but I'm fairly sure it was No. 13."

"*My!*"

The refreshment tent soon began to fill up again. The general opinion seemed to be that it was going to be a close race between No. 13 and No. 28, a red Omega car, driven by Marino, the Italian "ace."

"Dirtiest driver I ever seen," said one man with relish. "Why, over at Belfast 'e was just tipping 'em all into the ditches, just like winking."

"There's one thing you *can* be sure of. They won't *both* finish."

"It's sheer murder the way that Marino drives—a fair treat to see 'im."

"He's a one all right—a real artist and no mistake about it."

Adam and Miss Runcible and Archie and Miles went back to their pit.

"After all," said Miss Runcible, "the poor sweet may be wanting all sorts of things and signalling away

238

like mad, and no one there to pay any attention to him—so discouraging."

By this time the cars were fairly evenly spread out over the course. They flashed by intermittently with dazzling speed and a shriek; one or two drew into their pits and the drivers leapt out, trembling like leaves, to tinker with the works. One had already come to grief—a large German whose tyre had burst—punctured, some said, by a hireling of Marino's. It had left the road and shot up a tree like a cat chased by a dog. Two little American cars had failed to start; their team worked desperately at them amid derisive comments from the crowd. Suddenly two cars appeared coming down the straight, running abreast within two feet of each other.

"It's No. 13," cried Miss Runcible, really excited at last. "And there's that Italian devil just beside it. Come on, thirteen! Come on!" she cried, dancing in the pit and waving a flag she found at hand. "Come on. Oh! Well done, thirteen."

The cars were gone in a flash and succeeded by others.

"Agatha, darling, you shouldn't have waved the blue flag."

"My dear, how awful. Why not?"

"Well, that means that he's to stop next lap."

"Good God. Did I wave a blue flag?"

"My dear, you know you did."

"How shaming. What *am* I to say to him?"

"Let's all go away before he comes back."

"D'you know, I think we'd better. He might be furious, mightn't he? Let's go to the tent and have another drink—don't you think, or don't you?"

So No. 13 pit was again deserted.

"What did I say?" said the mechanic. "The moment I heard we'd drawn this blinkin' number I knew we was in for trouble."

The first person they saw when they reached the refreshment tent was the drunk Major.

"Your boy friend again," said Miles.

"Well, there you are," said the Major. "D'you know I've been chasing you all over London. What have you been doing with yourself all this time?"

"I've been staying at Lottie's."

"Well, she said she'd never heard of you. You see, I don't mind admitting I'd had a few too many that night, and to tell you the truth I woke up with things all rather a blur. Well then I found a thousand pounds in my pocket, and it all came back to me. There'd been a cove at Lottie's who gave me a thousand pounds to put on Indian Runner. Well, as far as I knew, Indian Runner was no good. I didn't want to lose your money for you, but the devil of it was I didn't know you from Adam." ("I think that's a perfect joke," said Miss Runcible.) "And apparently Lottie didn't either. You'd have thought it was easy enough to trace the sort of chap who deals out thousands of pounds to total strangers, but I couldn't find one finger-print."

"Do you mean," said Adam, a sudden delirious hope rising in his heart, "that you've still got my thousand?"

"Not so fast," said the Major. "I'm spinning this yarn. Well, on the day of the race I didn't know what to do. One half of me said, keep the thousand. The chap's bound to turn up some time, and it's his business to do his own punting—the other half said, put it on the favourite for him and give him a run for his money."

"So you put it on the favourite?" Adam's heart felt like lead again.

"No, I didn't. In the end I said, well, the young chap must be frightfully rich. If he likes to throw

241

away his money, it's none of my business, so I planked it all on Indian Runner for you."

"You mean . . ."

"I mean I've got the nice little packet of thirty-five thou. waiting until you condescend to call for it."

"Good heavens . . . look here, have a drink, won't you?"

"That's a thing I never refuse."

"Archie, lend me some money until I get this fortune."

"How much?"

"Enough to buy five bottles of champagne."

"Yes, if you can get them."

The barmaid had a case of champagne at the back of the tent. ("People often feel queer through watching the cars go by so fast—ladies especially," she explained.) So they took a bottle each and sat on the side of the hill and drank to Adam's prosperity.

"Hullo, everybody," said the loud speaker. "Car No. 28, the Italian Omega, driven by Captain Marino, has just completed the course in twelve minutes one second, lapping at an average speed of 78.3 miles per hour. This is the fastest time yet recorded."

A burst of applause greeted this announcement, but
242

Adam said, "I've rather lost interest in this race."

"Look here, old boy," the Major said when they were well settled down, "I'm in rather a hole. Makes me feel an awful ass, saying so, but the truth is I got my note-case pinched in the crowd. Of course, I've got plenty of small change to see me back to the hotel and they'll take a cheque of mine there, naturally, but the fact is I was keen to make a few bets with some chaps I hardly know. I wonder, old boy, could you possibly lend me a fiver? I can give it to you at the same time as I hand over the thirty-five thousand."

"Why, of course," said Adam. "Archie, lend me a fiver, can you?"

"Awfully good of you," said the Major, tucking the notes into his hip pocket. "Would it be all the same if you made it a tenner while we're about it?"

"I'm sorry," said Archie, with a touch of coldness. "I've only just got enough to get home with."

"That's all right, old boy, *I* understand. Not another word. . . . Well, here's to us all."

"I was on the course at the November Handicap," said Adam. "I thought I saw you."

"It would have saved a lot of fuss if we'd met, wouldn't it? Still, all's well that ends well."

243

"What an *angelic* man your Major is," said Miss Runcible.

When they had finished their champagne, the Major—now indisputably drunk—rose to go.

"Look here, old boy," he said. "I must be toddling along now. Got to see some chaps. Thanks no end for the binge. So jolly having met you all again. Bye-bye, little lady."

"When shall we meet again?" said Adam.

"Any time, old boy. Tickled to death to see you at any time you care to drop in. Always a pew and a drink for old friends. So long everybody."

"But couldn't I come and see you soon? About the money, you know."

"Sooner the better, old boy. Though I don't know what you mean about money."

"My thirty-five thousand."

"Why, yes, to be sure. Fancy my forgetting that. I tell you what. You roll along tonight to the Central and I'll give it to you then. Jolly glad to get it off my chest. Seven o'clock at the American bar—or a little before."

"Let's go back and look at the motor cars," said Archie.

They went down the hill feeling buoyant and detached (as one should if one drinks a great deal before luncheon). When they reached the pits they decided they were hungry. It seemed too far to climb up to the dining tent, so they ate as much of the mechanic's lunch as Miss Runcible's cigarette had spared.

Then a mishap happened to No. 13. It drew into the side uncertainly, with the mechanic holding the steering wheel. A spanner, he told them, thrown from Marino's car as they were passing him under the railway bridge, had hit Miles' friend on the shoulder. The mechanic helped him get out, and supported him to the Red Cross tent. "May as well scratch," he said. "He won't be good for anything more this afternoon. It's asking for trouble having a No. 13." Miles went to help his friend, leaving Miss Runcible and Adam and Archie staring rather stupidly at their motor car. Archie hiccoughed slightly as he ate the mechanic's apple.

Soon an official appeared.

"What happened here?" he said.

"Driver's just been murdered," said Archie. "Spanner under the railway bridge. Marino."

"Well, are you going to scratch? Who's spare driver?"

245

"I don't know. Do you, Adam? I shouldn't be a bit surprised if they hadn't murdered the spare driver, too."

"I'm spare driver," said Miss Runcible. "It's on my arm."

"She's spare driver. Look, it's on her arm."

"Well, do you want to scratch?"

"Don't you scratch, Agatha."

"No, I don't want to scratch."

"All right. What's your name?"

"Agatha. I'm the spare driver. It's on my arm."

"I can see it is—all right, start off as soon as you like."

"Agatha," repeated Miss Runcible firmly as she climbed into the car. "It's on my arm."

"I say, Agatha," said Adam. "Are you sure you're all right?"

"It's on my arm," said Miss Runcible severely.

"I mean, are you quite certain it's absolutely safe?"

"Not *absolutely* safe, Adam. Not if they throw spanners. But I'll go quite slowly at first until I'm used to it. Just you see. Coming too?"

"I'll stay and wave the flag," said Adam.

"That's right. Good-bye . . . goodness, how too stiff-scaring. . . ."

246

The car shot out into the middle of the road, missed a collision by a foot, swung round and disappeared with a roar up the road.

"I say, Archie, is it all right being tight in a car, if it's on a race course? They won't run her in or anything?"

"No, no, that's all right. All tight on the race course."

"Sure?"

"Sure."

"All of them?"

"Absolutely everyone—tight as houses."

"That's all right then. Let's go and have a drink."

So they went up the hill again, through the Boy Scouts, to the refreshment tent.

It was not long before Miss Runcible was in the news.

"Hullo, everybody," said the loud speaker. "No. 13, the English Plunket-Bowse, driven by Miss Agatha, came into collision at Headlong Corner with No. 28, the Italian Omega car, driven by Captain Marino. No. 13 righted itself and continued on the course. No. 28 overturned and has retired from the race."

"Well done, Agatha," said Archie.

A few minutes later:

"Hullo, everybody. No. 13, the English Plunket-Bowse, driven by Miss Agatha, has just completed the course in nine minutes forty-one seconds. This constitutes a record for the course."

Patriotic cheers broke out on all sides, and Miss Runcible's health was widely drunk in the refreshment tent.

A few minutes later:

"Hullo, everybody; I have to contradict the announcement recently made that No. 13, the English Plunket-Bowse, driven by Miss Agatha, had established a record for the course. The stewards have now reported that No. 13 left the road just after the level crossing and cut across country for five miles, rejoining the track at the Red Lion corner. The lap has therefore been disallowed by the judges."

A few minutes later:

"Hullo, everybody; No. 13, the English Plunket-Bowse car, driven by Miss Agatha, has retired from the race. It disappeared from the course some time ago, turning left instead of right at Church Corner, and was last seen proceeding south on the bye-road, apparently out of control."

"My dear, that's lucky for me," said Miles. "A

really good story my second day on the paper. This ought to do me good with the *Excess—very* rich-making," and he hurried off to the post-office tent—which was one of the amenities of the course—to despatch a long account of Miss Runcible's disaster.

Adam accompanied him and sent a wire to Nina: *"Drunk Major in refreshment tent not bogus thirty-five thousand married tomorrow everything perfect Agatha lost love Adam."*

"That seems quite clear," he said.

They went to the hospital tent after this—another amenity of the course—to see how Miles' friend was getting on. He seemed in some pain and showed anxiety about his car.

"I think it's very heartless of him," said Adam. "He ought to be worried about Agatha. It only shows . . ."

"Motor men *are* heartless," said Miles, with a sigh.

Presently Captain Marino was borne in on a stretcher. He turned on his side with a deep groan and spat at Miles' friend as he went past him. He also spat at the doctor who came to bandage him and bit one of the V.A.D.'s.

They said Captain Marino was no gentleman in the hospital tent.

There was no chance of leaving the course before the end of the race, Archie was told, and the race would not be over for at least two hours. Round and round went the stream of cars. At intervals the Boy Scouts posted a large red R against one or other of the numbers, as engine trouble or collision or Headlong Corner took its toll. A long queue stretched along the top of the hill from the door of the luncheon tent. Then it began to rain.

There was nothing for it but to go back to the bar.

At dusk the last car completed its course. The silver gilt trophy was presented to the winner. The loud speaker broadcast "God Save the King," and a cheerful "Good-bye, everybody." The tail of the queue outside the dining tent were respectfully informed that no more luncheons could be served. The barmaids in the refreshment tent said, "All glasses, ladies and gentlemen, please." The motor ambulances began a final round of the track to pick up survivors. Then Adam and Miles and Archie Schwert went to look for their car.

Darkness fell during the drive back. It took an hour to reach the town. Adam and Miles and Archie Schwert did not talk much. The effect of their drinks had now entered on that secondary stage, vividly described in temperance hand-books, when the momentary illusion of well-being and exhilaration gives place to melancholy, indigestion and moral decay. Adam tried to concentrate his thoughts upon his sudden wealth, but they seemed unable to adhere to this high pinnacle, and as often as he impelled them up, slithered back helplessly to his present physical discomfort.

The sluggish procession in which they were moving led them eventually to the centre of the town and the soberly illuminated front of the Imperial Hotel. A torrential flow of wet and hungry motor enthusiasts swept and eddied about the revolving doors.

"I shall die if I don't eat something soon," said Miles. "Let's leave Agatha until we've had a meal."

But the manager of the "Imperial" was unimpressed by numbers or necessity and manfully upheld the integrity of British hotel-keeping. Tea, he explained, was served daily in the Palm Court with orchestra on Thursdays and Sundays between the hours of four and six. A *table d'hôte* dinner was served in the dining-room from seven-thirty until nine o'clock. An *à la carte* dinner was also served in the grill room at the same time. It was now twenty minutes past six. If the gentlemen cared to return in an hour and ten

251

minutes he would do his best to accommodate them, but he could not promise to reserve a table. Things were busy that day. There had been motor races in the neighbourhood, he explained.

The commissionaire was more helpful, and told them that there was a tea-shop restaurant called the Café Royal a little way down the High Street, next to the Cinema. He seemed, however, to have given the same advice to all comers, for the Café Royal was crowded and overflowing. Everyone was being thoroughly cross, but only the most sarcastic and overbearing were given tables, and only the gross and outrageous were given food. Adam and Miles and Archie Schwert then tried two more tea-shops, one kept by "ladies" and called "The Honest Injun," a workmen's dining-room and a fried-fish shop. Eventually they bought a bag of mixed biscuits at a co-operative store, which they ate in the Palm Court of the "Imperial," maintaining a moody silence.

It was now after seven, and Adam remembered his appointment in the American bar. There, too, inevitably, was a dense crowd. Some of the "Speed Kings" themselves had appeared, pink from their baths, wearing dinner-jackets and stiff white shirts,

252

each in his circle of admirers. Adam struggled to the bar.

"Have you seen a drunk major in here anywhere?" he asked.

The barmaid sniffed. "I should think not, indeed," she said. "And I shouldn't serve him if he *did* come in. I don't have people of that description in *my* bar. *The very idea.*"

"Well, perhaps he's not drunk now. But have you seen a stout, red-faced man, with a single eyeglass and a turned-up moustache?"

"Well, there *was* someone like that not so long ago. Are you a friend of his?"

"I want to see him badly."

"Well, all I can say is I wish you'd try and look after him and don't bring him in here again. Going on something awful he was. Broke two glasses and got very quarrelsome with the other gentlemen. He had three or four pound notes in his hand. Kept waving them about and saying, 'D'you know what? I met a mutt today. I owe him thirty-five thousand pounds and he lent me a fiver.' Well, that's not the way to talk before strangers, is it? He went out ten minutes ago. I was glad to see the back of him, I can tell you."

253

"Did he say that—about having met a mutt?"

"Didn't stop saying it the whole time he was in here —most monotonous."

But as Adam left the bar he saw the Major coming out of the gentlemen's lavatory. He was walking very deliberately, and stared at Adam with a glazed and vacant eye.

"Hi!" cried Adam. "Hi!"

"Cheerio," said the drunk Major distantly.

"I say," said Adam. "What about my thirty-five thousand pounds?"

The drunk Major stopped and adjusted his monocle.

"Thirty-five thousand and five pounds," he said. "What about them?"

"Well, where are they?"

"They're safe enough. National and Provincial Union Bank of England, Limited. A perfectly sound and upright company. I'd trust them with more than that if I had it. I'd trust them with a million, old boy, honest I would. One of those fine old companies, you know. They don't make companies like that now. I'd trust that bank with my wife and kiddies. . . .

254

You mustn't think I'd put your money into anything that wasn't straight, old boy. You ought to know me well enough for that. . . ."

"No, of course not. It's terribly kind of you to have looked after it—you said you'd give me a cheque this evening. Don't you remember?"

The drunk Major looked at him craftily. "Ah," he said. "That's another matter. I told *someone* I'd give him a cheque. But how am I to know it was you? . . . I've got to be careful, you know. Suppose you were just a crook dressed up. I don't say you are, mind, but supposing. Where'd I be then? You have to look at both sides of a case like this."

"Oh, God. . . . I've got two friends here who'll swear to you I'm Adam Symes. Will that do?"

"Might be a gang. Besides *I* don't know that the name of the chap who gave me the thousand *was* Adam what-d'you-call-it at all. Only your word for it. I'll tell you what," said the Major, sitting down in a deep armchair, "I'll sleep on it. Just forty winks. I'll let you know my decision when I wake up. Don't think me suspicious, old boy, but I've got to be careful . . . other chap's money, you know . . ." And he fell asleep.

Adam struggled through the crowd to the Palm

255

Court, where he had left Miles and Archie. News of No. 13 had just come through. The car had been found piled up on the market cross of a large village about fifteen miles away (doing irreparable damage to a monument already scheduled for preservation by the Office of Works). But there was no sign of Miss Runcible.

"I suppose we ought to do something about it," said Miles. "This is the most miserable day I ever spent. Did you get your fortune?"

"The Major was too drunk to recognize me. He's just gone to sleep."

"*Well.*"

"We must go to this beastly village and look for Agatha."

"I can't leave my Major. He'll probably wake up soon and give the fortune to the first person he sees."

"Let's just go and shake him until he gives us the fortune now," said Miles.

But this was impracticable, for when they reached the chair where Adam had left him, the drunk Major was gone.

The hall porter remembered him going out quite clearly. He had pressed a pound into his hand, saying, "Met-a-mutt-today," and taken a taxi to the station.

256

"D'you know," said Adam, "I don't believe that I'm ever going to get that fortune."

"Well, I don't see that you've very much to complain of," said Archie. "You're no worse off than you were. *I've* lost a fiver and five bottles of champagne."

"That's true," said Adam, a little consoled.

They got into the car and drove through the rain to the village where the Plunket-Bowse had been found. There it stood, still smoking and partially recognizable, surrounded by admiring villagers. A constable in a waterproof cape was doing his best to preserve it intact from the raids of souvenir hunters who were collecting the smaller fragments.

No one seemed to have witnessed the disaster. The younger members of the community were all at the races, while the elders were engaged in their afternoon naps. One thought he had heard a crash.

Inquiries at the railway station, however, disclosed that a young lady, much dishevelled in appearance, and wearing some kind of band on her arm, had appeared in the booking office early that afternoon and asked where she was. On being told, she said, well, she wished she wasn't, because someone had left an enormous stone spanner in the middle of the road. She

257

admitted feeling rather odd. The station-master had asked her if she would like to come in and sit down and offered to get her some brandy. She said, "No, no more brandy," and bought a first-class ticket to London. She had left on the 3.25 train.

"So that's all right," said Archie.

Then they left the village and presently found an hotel on the Great North Road, where they dined and spent the night. They reached London by luncheon time next day, and learned that Miss Runcible had been found early that morning staring fixedly at a model engine in the central hall at Euston Station. In answer to some gentle questions, she replied that to the best of her knowledge she had no name, pointing to the brassard on her arm, as if in confirmation of this fact. She had come in a motor car, she explained, which would not stop. It was full of bugs which she had tried to kill with drops of face lotion. One of them threw a spanner. There had been a stone thing in the way. They shouldn't put up symbols like that in the middle of the road, should they, or should they?

So they conveyed her to a nursing home in Wimpole Street and kept her for some time in a darkened room.

XI

DAM rang up Nina.

"Darling, I've been so happy about your telegram. Is it really true?"

"No, I'm afraid not."

"The Major *is* bogus?"

"Yes."

"You haven't got any money?"

"No."

"We aren't going to be married today?"

"No."

"I see."

"Well?"

"I said, I see."

"Is that all?"

"Yes, that's all, Adam."

"I'm sorry."

"I'm sorry, too. Good-bye."

259

"Good-bye, Nina."

Later Nina rang up Adam.

"Darling, is that you? I've got something rather awful to tell you."

"Yes?"

"You'll be furious."

"Well?"

"I'm engaged to be married."

"Who to?"

"I hardly think I can tell you."

"Who?"

"Adam, you won't be beastly about it, will you?"

"Who is it?"

"Ginger."

"I don't believe it."

"Well, I am. That's all there is to it."

"You're going to marry Ginger?"

"Yes."

"I see."

"Well?"

"I said, I see."

"Is that all?"

"Yes, that's all, Nina."

"When shall I see you?"

"I don't want ever to see you again."

"I see."
"Well?"
"I said, I see."
"Well, good-bye."
"Good-bye. . . . I'm sorry, Adam."

XII

EN days later Adam bought some flowers at the corner of Wigmore Street and went to call on Miss Runcible at her nursing home. He was shown first into the matron's room. She had numerous photographs in silver frames and a very nasty fox terrier. She smoked a cigarette in a greedy way, making slight sucking noises.

"Just taking a moment off in my den," she explained. "Down, Spot, down. But I can see you're fond of dogs," she added, as Adam gave Spot a half-hearted pat on the head. "So you want to see Miss Runcible? Well, I ought to warn you first that she must have no kind of excitement whatever. She's had a severe shock. Are you a relation, may I ask?"

"No, only a friend."

"A very *special* friend, perhaps, eh?" said the Matron archly. "Never mind, I'll spare your blushes.

Just you run up and see her. But not more than five minutes, mind, or you'll have me on your tracks."

There was a reek of ether on the stairs which reminded Adam of the times when, waiting to take her to luncheon, he had sat on Nina's bed while she did her face. (She invariably made him turn his back until it was over, having a keen sense of modesty about this one part of her toilet, in curious contrast to some girls, who would die rather than be seen in their underclothes, and yet openly flaunt unpainted faces in front of anyone.)

It hurt Adam deeply to think much about Nina.

Outside Miss Runcible's door hung a very interesting chart which showed the fluctuations of her temperature and pulse and many other curious details of her progress. He studied this with pleasure until a nurse, carrying a tray of highly polished surgical instruments, gave him such a look that he felt obliged to turn away.

Miss Runcible lay in a high, narrow bed in a darkened room.

A nurse was crocheting at her side when Adam entered. She rose, dropping a few odds and ends from her lap, and said, "There's someone come to see you, dear. Now remember you aren't to talk much." She took the flowers from Adam's hand, said, "Look what lovelies. Aren't you a lucky girl?" and left the room with them. She returned a moment later carrying them in a jug of water. "There, the thirsties," she said. "Don't they love to get back to the nice cool water?"

Then she went out again.

"Darling," said a faint voice from the bed, "I can't really see who it is. Would it be awful to draw the curtains?"

Adam crossed the room and let in the light of the grey December afternoon.

"My dear, how blind-making. There are some cock-tail things in the wardrobe. Do make a big one. The nurses love them so. It's such a nice nursing home this, Adam, only all the nurses are starved, and there's a breath-taking young man next door who keeps putting his head in and asking how I am. *He* fell out of an *aeroplane*, which is rather grand, don't you think?"

"How are you feeling, Agatha?"

"Well, rather odd, to tell you the truth. . . . How's Nina?"

"She's got engaged to be married—haven't you heard?"

"My dear, the nurses are interested in no one but Princess Elizabeth. Do tell me."

264

"A young man called Ginger."

"*Well?*"

"Don't you remember him? He came on with us after the airship party."

"Not the one who was sick?"

"No, the other."

"I don't remember . . . does Nina call him Ginger?"

"Yes."

"Why?"

"He asked her to."

"*Well?*"

"She used to play with him when they were children. So she's going to marry him."

"My dear, isn't that rather sad-making for you?"

"I'm desperate about it. I'm thinking of committing suicide, like Simon."

"Don't do that, darling . . . did Simon commit suicide?"

"My dear, you know he did. The night all those libel actions started."

"Oh, *that* Simon. I thought you meant *Simon.*"

"Who's Simon?"

"The young man who fell out of the aeroplane. The nurses call him Simple Simon because it's affected his

265

brains . . . but, Adam, I *am* sorry about Nina. I'll tell you what we'll do. As soon as I'm well again we'll make Mary Mouse give a lovely party to cheer you up."

"Haven't you heard about Mary?"

"No, what?"

"She went off to Monte Carlo with the Maharajah of Pukkapore."

"*My dear,* aren't the Mice furious?"

"She's just receiving religious instruction before her official reception as a royal concubine. Then they're going to India."

"How people are *disappearing,* Adam. Did you get that money from the drunk Major?"

"No, he disappeared too."

"D'you know, all that time when I was dotty I had the most awful dreams. I thought we were all driving round and round in a motor race and none of us could stop, and there was an enormous audience composed entirely of gossip writers and gate crashers and Archie Schwert and people like that, all shouting at us at once to go faster, and car after car kept crashing until I was left all alone driving and driving—and then I used to crash and wake up."

Then the door opened, and Miles came popping in.

"Agatha, Adam, my dears. The *time* I've had trying to get in. I can't tell you how bogus they were downstairs. First I said I was Lord Chasm, and that wasn't any good; and I said I was one of the doctors, and that wasn't any good; and I said I was your young man, and *that* wasn't any good; and I said I was a gossip writer, and they let me up at once and said I wasn't to excite you, but would I put a piece in my paper about their nursing home. *How* are you, Aggie darling? I brought up some new records."

"You are angelic. Do let's try them. There's a gramophone under the bed."

"There's a whole lot more people coming to see you today. I saw them all at luncheon at Margot's. Johnny Hoop and Van and Archie Schwert. I wonder if they'll all manage to get in."

They got in.

So soon there was quite a party, and Simon appeared from next door in a very gay dressing-gown, and they played the new records and Miss Runcible moved her bandaged limbs under the bed-clothes in negro rhythm.

Last of all, Nina came in looking quite lovely and very ill.

"Nina, I hear you're engaged."

267

"Yes, it's very lucky. My papa has just put all his money into a cinema film and lost it all."

"My dear, it doesn't matter at all. My papa lost all his twice. It doesn't make a bit of difference. That's just one of the things one has to learn about losing all one's money. . . . Is it true that you really call him Ginger?"

"Well, yes, only, Agatha, please don't be unkind about it."

And the gramophone was playing the song which the black man sang at the Café de la Paix.

Then the nurse came in.

"Well, you are noisy ones, and no mistake," she said. "I don't know what the matron would say if she were here."

"Have a chocolate, sister?"

"*Ooh, chocs!*"

Adam made another cocktail.

Miles sat on Miss Runcible's bed and took up the telephone and began dictating some paragraphs about the nursing home.

"What it is to have a friend in the Press," said the nurse.

Adam brought her a cocktail. "Shall I?" she said. "I hope you haven't made it too strong. Suppose it goes to my head. What would the patients think if their sister came in tiddly? Well, if you're *sure* it won't hurt me, thanks."

". . . *Yesterday I visited the Hon. Agatha Runcible comma Lord Chasm's lovely daughter comma at the Wimpole Street nursing home where she is recovering from the effects of the motor accident recently described in this column stop. Miss Runcible was entertaining quite a large party which included . . .*"

Adam, handing round cocktails, came to Nina.

"I thought we were never going to meet each other again."

"We were obviously bound to, weren't we?"

"Agatha's looking better than I expected, isn't she? What an amusing nursing home."

"Nina, I must see you again. Come back to Lottie's this evening and have dinner with me."

"No."

"Please."

"No. Ginger wouldn't like it."

"Nina, you aren't in love with him?"

"No, I don't think so."

"Are you in love with me?"

"I don't know . . . I was once."

"Nina, I'm absolutely miserable not seeing you. Do

269

come and dine with me tonight. What can be the harm in that?"

"My dear, I know exactly what it will mean."

"Well, why not?"

"You see, Ginger's not like us really about that sort of thing. He'd be furious."

"Well, what about me? Surely I have first claim?"

"Darling, don't *bully*. Besides, I used to play with Ginger as a child. His hair was a very pretty colour then."

". . . *Mr. 'Johnny' Hoop, whose memoirs are to be published next month, told me that he intends to devote his time to painting in future, and is going to Paris to study in the spring. He is to be taken into the studio of . . ."*

"For the last time, Nina . . ."

"Well, I suppose I must."

"*Angel!*"

"I believe you knew I was going to."

". . . *Miss Nina Blount, whose engagement to Mr. 'Ginger' Littlejohn, the well-known polo player. . . . Mr. Schwert . . ."*

"If only you were as rich as Ginger, Adam, or only half as rich. Or if only you had any money at all."

"Well," said the Matron, appearing suddenly. "Whoever heard of cocktails and a gramophone in a concussion case? Sister Briggs, pull down those curtains at once. Out you go, the whole lot of you. Why, I've known cases die with less."

Indeed, Miss Runcible was already showing signs of strain. She was sitting bolt upright in bed, smiling deliriously, and bowing her bandaged head to imaginary visitors.

"*Darling*," she said. "How *too* divine . . . *how* are you? . . . and how are *you?* . . . how angelic of you all to come . . . only you must be careful not to fall out at the corners . . . ooh, just missed it. There goes that nasty Italian car . . . I wish I knew which thing was which in this car . . . darling, do try and drive more straight, my sweet, you were nearly into me then. . . . Faster . . ."

"That's all right, Miss Runcible, that's all right. You mustn't get excited," said the Matron. "Sister Briggs, run for the ice-pack quickly."

"All friends here," said Miss Runcible, smiling radiantly. "Faster. . . . Faster . . . it'll stop all right when the times comes . . ."

That evening Miss Runcible's temperature went rocketing up the chart in a way which aroused great interest throughout the nursing home. Sister Briggs over her evening cup of cocoa said she would be sorry to lose that case. Such a nice bright girl—but terribly excitable.

At Shepheard's Hotel Lottie said to Adam:

"That chap's been in here again after you."

"What chap, Lottie?"

"How do I know what chap? Same chap as before."

"You never told me about a chap."

"Didn't I, dear? Well, I meant to."

"What did he want?"

"I don't know—something about money. Dun, I expect. Says he is coming back tomorrow."

"Well, tell him I've gone to Manchester."

"That's right, dear. . . . What about a glass of wine?"

Later that evening Nina said: "You don't seem to be enjoying yourself very much tonight."

"Sorry, am I being a bore?"

"I think I shall go home."

"Yes."

272

"Adam, darling, what's the matter?"

"I don't know. . . . Nina, do you ever feel that things simply can't go on much longer?"

"What d'you mean by things—us or everything?"

"Everything."

"No—I wish I did."

"I dare say you're right . . . what are you looking for?"

"Clothes."

"Why?"

"Oh, Adam, what *do* you want . . . you're too impossible this evening."

"Don't let's talk any more, Nina, d'you mind?"

Later he said: "I'd give anything in the world for something different."

"Different from me or different from everything?"

"Different from everything . . . only I've got nothing . . . what's the good of talking?"

"Oh, Adam, my dearest . . ."

"Yes?"

"Nothing."

When Adam came down next morning Lottie was having her morning glass of champagne in the parlour.

"So your little bird's flown, has she? Sit down and have a glass of wine. That dun's been in again. I told him you was in Manchester."

"Splendid."

"Seemed rather shirty about it. Said he'd go and look for you."

"Better still."

Then something happened which Adam had been dreading for days. Lottie suddenly said:

"And that reminds me. What about *my* little bill?"

"Oh, yes," said Adam, "I've been meaning to ask for it. Have it made out and sent up to me some time, will you?"

"I've got it here. Bless you, what a lot you seem to have drunk."

"Yes, I do, don't I? Are you sure some of this champagne wasn't the Judge's?"

"Well, it may have been," admitted Lottie. "We get a bit muddled with the books now and then."

"Well, thank you so much, I'll send you down a cheque for this."

"No, dear," said Lottie. "Suppose you write it down here. Here's the pen, here's the ink, and here's a blank cheque book."

(Bills are delivered infrequently and irregularly at

274

Lottie's, but when they come, there is no getting away from them.) Adam wrote out a cheque for seventy-eight pounds sixteen shillings.

"And twopence for the cheque," said Lottie.

And twopence, Adam added.

"There's a dear," said Lottie, blotting the cheque and locking it away in a drawer. "Why look who's turned up. If it isn't Mr. Thingummy."

It was Ginger.

"Good morning, Mrs. Crump," he said rather stiffly.

"Come and sit down and have a glass of wine, dear. Why I knew you before you were born."

"Hullo, Ginger," said Adam.

"Look here, Symes," said Ginger, looking in an embarrassed manner at the glass of champagne which had been put into his hand, "I want to speak to you. Perhaps we can go somewhere where we shan't be disturbed."

"Bless you, boys, I won't disturb you," said Lottie. "Just you have a nice talk. I've got lots to see to."

She left the parlour, and soon her voice could be heard raised in anger against the Italian waiter.

"Well?" said Adam.

"Look here, Symes," said Ginger, "what I mean to say is, what I'm going to say may sound damned unpleasant, you know, and all that, but look here, you know, damn it, I mean *the better man won*—not that I mean I'm the *better* man. Wouldn't say that for a minute. And anyway, Nina's a damn sight too good for either of us. It's just that I've been lucky. Awful rough luck on you, I mean, and all that, but still, when you come to think of it, after all, well, look here, damn it, I mean, d'you see what I mean?"

"Not quite," said Adam gently. "Now tell me again. Is it something about Nina?"

"Yes, it is," said Ginger in a rush. "Nina and I are engaged, and I'm not going to have you butting in or there'll be hell to pay." He paused, rather taken aback at his own eloquence.

"What makes you think I'm butting in?"

"Well, hang it all, she dined with you last night, didn't she, and stayed out jolly late, too."

"How do you know how late she stayed out?"

"Well, as a matter of fact, you see I wanted to speak to her about something rather important, so I rang her up once or twice and didn't get an answer until three o'clock."

"I suppose you rang her up about every ten minutes?"

"Oh, no, damn it, not as often as that," said Ginger.

276

"No, no, not as often as that. I know it sounds rather unsporting and all that, but you see I wanted to speak to her, and, anyway, when I did get through, she just said she had a pain and didn't want to talk; *well, I mean to say.* After all, I mean, one is a gentleman. It isn't as though you were just a sort of friend of the family, is it? I mean, you were more or less engaged to her yourself, weren't you, at one time? Well, what would you have thought if I'd come butting in? You must look at it like that, from my point of view, too, mustn't you, I mean?"

"Well, I think that's rather what did happen."

"Oh, no, look here, Symes, I mean, damn it; you mustn't say things like that. D'you know all the time I was out East I had Nina's photograph over my bed, honest I did. I expect you think that's sentimental and all that, but what I mean is I didn't stop thinking of that girl once all the time I was away. Mind you, there were lots of other frightfully jolly girls out there, and I don't say I didn't sometimes get jolly pally with them, you know, tennis and gymkhana and all that sort of thing, I mean, and dancing in the evenings, but never anything serious, you know. Nina was the only girl I really thought of, and I'd sort of made up my mind when I came home to look her up, and if she'd

277

have me . . . see what I mean? So you see it's awfully rough luck on me when someone comes butting in. You must see that, don't you?"

"Yes," said Adam.

"And there's another thing, you know, sentiment and all that apart. I mean Nina's a girl who likes nice clothes and things, you know, comfort and all that. Well, I mean to say, of course, her father's a topping old boy, absolutely one of the best, but he's rather an ass about money, if you know what I mean. What I mean, Nina's going to be frightfully hard up, and all that, and I mean you haven't got an awful lot of money, have you?"

"I haven't any at all."

"No, I mean, that's what I mean. *Awfully rough on you.* No one thinks the worse of you, respects you for it, I mean earning a living and all that. Heaps of fellows haven't any money nowadays. I could give you the names of dozens of stout fellows, absolute toppers, who simply haven't a bean. No, all I mean is, when it comes to marrying, then that does make a difference, doesn't it?"

"What you've been trying to say all this time is that you're not sure of Nina?"

"Oh, rot, my dear fellow, absolute bilge. Damn it,
278

I'd trust Nina anywhere, of course I would. After all, damn it, what does being in love mean if you can't trust a person?"

("What, indeed?" thought Adam), and he said, "Now, Ginger, tell the truth. What's Nina worth to you?"

"Good Lord, why what an extraordinary thing to ask; everything in the world, of course. I'd go through fire and water for that girl."

"Well, I'll sell her to you."

"No, why, look here, good God, damn it, I mean . . ."

"I'll sell you my share in her for a hundred pounds."

"You pretend to be fond of Nina and you talk about her like that! Why, hang it, it's not decent. Besides, a hundred pounds is the deuce of a lot. I mean, getting married is a damned expensive business, don't you know. And I'm just getting a couple of polo ponies over from Ireland. That's going to cost a hell of a lot, what with one thing and another."

"A hundred down, and I leave Nina to you. I think it's cheap."

"Fifty."

"A hundred."

"Seventy-five."

"A hundred."

"I'm damned if I'll pay more than seventy-five."

"I'll take seventy-eight pounds sixteen and two-pence. I can't go lower than that."

"All right, I'll pay that. *You really will go away?*"

"I'll try, Ginger. Have a drink."

"No, thank you . . . this only shows what an escape Nina's had—poor little girl."

"Good-bye, Ginger."

"Good-bye, Symes."

"Young Thingummy going?" said Lottie, appearing in the door. "I was just thinking about a little drink."

Adam went to the telephone-box. . . . "Hullo, is that Nina?"

"Who's speaking, please? I don't think Miss Blount is in."

"Mr. Fenwick-Symes."

"Oh, Adam. I was afraid it was Ginger. I woke up feeling I just couldn't bear him. He rang up last night just as I got in."

"I know. Nina, darling, something awful's happened."

"What?"

280

"Lottie presented me with her bill."

"Darling, what *did* you do?"

"Well, I did something rather extraordinary. . . . My dear, I sold *you.*"

"Darling . . . *who to?*"

"Ginger. You fetched seventy-eight pounds sixteen and twopence."

"Well?"

"And now I never am going to see you again."

"Oh, but Adam, I think this is beastly of you. I don't want not to see you again."

"I'm sorry. . . . Good-bye, Nina, darling."

"Good-bye, Adam, my sweet. But I think you're rather a cad."

Next day Lottie said to Adam, "You know that chap I said came here asking for you?"

"The dun?"

"Well, he wasn't a dun. I've just remembered. He's a chap who used to come here quite a lot until he had a fight with a Canadian. He was here the night that silly Flossie killed herself on the chandelier."

"Not the drunk Major?"

"He wasn't drunk yesterday. Not so as you'd no-

281

tice anyway. Red-faced chap with an eyeglass. You ought to remember him, dear. He was the one made that bet for you on the November Handicap."

"But I must get hold of him at once. What's his name?"

"Ah, that I couldn't tell you. I *did* know, but it's slipped my memory. He's gone to Manchester to look for you. Pity your missing him!"

Then Adam rang up Nina. "Listen," he said. "Don't do anything sudden about Ginger. I may be able to buy you back. The drunk Major has turned up again."

"But, darling, it's too late. Ginger and I got married this morning. I'm just packing for our honeymoon. We're going in an aeroplane."

"Ginger wasn't taking any chances, was he? Darling, don't go."

"No, I must. Ginger says he knows a 'top-hole little spot not far from Monte with a very decent nine-hole golf course.' "

"*Well?*"

"*Yes, I know* . . . we shall only be away a few days. We're coming back to spend Christmas with papa. Perhaps we shall be able to arrange something when we get back. I do hope so."

282

"Good-bye."
"Good-bye."

Ginger looked out of the aeroplane: "I say, Nina," he shouted, "when you were young did you ever have to learn a thing out of a poetry book about: *'This scepter'd isle, this earth of majesty, this something or other Eden'*? D'you know what I mean? *'this happy breed of men, this little world, this precious stone set in the silver sea. . . .*

"*'This blessed plot, this earth, this realm, this England*
This nurse, this teeming womb of royal kings
Feared by their breed and famous by their birth . . .'

"I forget how it goes on. Something about a stubborn Jew. But you know the thing I mean?"

"It comes in a play."

"No, a blue poetry book."

"I acted in it."

"Well, they may have put it into a play since. It was in a blue poetry book when I learned it. Anyway, you know what I mean?"

"Yes, why?"

"Well, I mean to say, don't you feel somehow, up

283

in the air like this and looking down and seeing everything underneath. I mean, don't you have a sort of feeling rather like that, if you see what I mean?"

Nina looked down and saw inclined at an odd angle a horizon of straggling red suburb; arterial roads dotted with little cars; factories, some of them working, others empty and decaying; a disused canal; some distant hills sown with bungalows; wireless masts and overhead power cables; men and women were indiscernible except as tiny spots; they were marrying and shopping and making money and having children. The scene lurched and tilted again as the aeroplane struck a current of air.

"I think I'm going to be sick," said Nina.

"Poor little girl," said Ginger. "That's what the paper bags are for."

There was rarely more than a quarter of a mile of the black road to be seen at one time. It unrolled like a length of cinema film. At the edges was confusion; a fog spinning past; *"Faster, faster,"* they shouted above the roar of the engine. The road rose suddenly and the white car soared up the sharp ascent without slackening of speed. At the summit of the hill there was a corner. Two cars had crept up, one on each side, and were closing in. "Faster," cried Miss Runcible. "Faster."

"Quietly, dear, quietly. You're disturbing everyone. You must lie quiet or you'll never get well. Everything's quite all right. There's nothing to worry about. Nothing at all."

They were trying to make her lie down. How could one drive properly lying down?

Another frightful corner. The car leant over on two wheels, tugging outwards; it was drawn across the road until it was within a few inches of the bank. One ought to brake down at the corners, but one couldn't see them coming lying flat on one's back like this. The back wheels wouldn't hold the road at this speed. Skidding all over the place.

"Faster. Faster."

The stab of a hypodermic needle.

"There's nothing to worry about, dear . . . *nothing at all . . . nothing.*"

XIII

HE film had been finished, and everyone had gone away; Wesley and Whitefield, Bishop Philpotts and Miss La Touche, Mr. Isaacs, and all his pupils from the National Academy of Cinematographic Art. The park lay deep in snow, a clean expanse of white, shadowless and unspotted save for tiny broad arrows stamped by the hungry birds. The bell-ringers were having their final practice, and the air was alive with pealing bells.

Inside the dining-room Florin and Mrs. Florin and Ada, the fifteen-year-old housemaid, were arranging branches of holly above the frames of the family portraits. Florin held the basket, Mrs. Florin held the steps and Ada put the decorations in their places. Colonel Blount was having his afternoon nap upstairs.

Florin had a secret. It was a white calico banner of

286

great age lettered in red ribbon with the words "WEL-
COME HOME." He had always known where it was, just
where to put his hand on it, at the top of the black
trunk in the far attic behind the two hip baths and
the 'cello case.

"The Colonel's mother made it," he explained,
"when he first went away to school, and it was always
hung out in the hall whenever he and Mister Eric
came back for the holidays. It used to be the first
thing he'd look for when he came into the house—
even when he was a grown man home on leave.
'Where's my banner?' he'd say. We'll have it up for
Miss Nina—Mrs. Littlejohn, I should say."

Ada said should they put some holly in Captain
and Mrs. Littlejohn's bedroom.

Mrs. Florin said, whoever heard of holly in a bedroom, and she wasn't sure but that it was unlucky to
take it upstairs.

Ada said, "Well, perhaps just a bit of mistletoe
over the bed."

Mrs. Florin said Ada was too young to think about
things like that, and she ought to be ashamed of herself.

Florin said would Ada stop arguing and answering
back and come into the hall to put up the banner.

One string went on the nose of the rhinoceros, he explained, the other round the giraffe.

Presently Colonel Blount came down.

"Should I light the fires in the big drawing-room?" asked Mrs. Florin.

"Fires in the big drawing-room? No, why should you want to do that, Mrs. Florin?"

"Because of Captain and Mrs. Littlejohn—you haven't forgotten, have you, sir, that they're coming to stay this afternoon?"

"Captain and Mrs. Fiddlesticks. Never heard of them. Who asked them to stay, I should like to know? *I* didn't. Don't know who they are. Don't want them. . . . Besides, now I come to think of it, Miss Nina and her husband said they were coming down. I can't have the whole house turned into an hotel. If these people come, Florin, whoever they are, you tell them to go away. You understand? I won't have them, and I think it's very presumptuous of whoever asked them. It is not their place to invite guests here without consulting me."

"Should I be lighting the fires in the big drawing-room for Miss Nina and her young gentleman, sir?"

"Yes, yes, certainly . . . and a fire in their bedroom, of course. And, Florin, I want you to come down to the cellar with me to look out some port . . . I've got the keys here. . . . I have a feeling I'm going to like Miss Nina's husband," he confided on their way to the cellar. "I hear very good reports of him—a decent, steady young fellow, and not at all badly off. Miss Nina said in her letter that he used to come over here as a little boy. D'you remember him, Florin? Blest if I do. . . . What's the name again?"

"Littlejohn, sir."

"Yes. Littlejohn, to be sure. I had the name on the tip of my tongue only a minute ago. *Littlejohn*. I must remember that."

"His father used to live over at Oakshott, sir. A very wealthy gentleman. Shipowners, I think they were. Young Mr. Littlejohn used to go riding with Miss Nina, sir. Regular little monkey he was, sir, red-headed . . . a terrible one for cats."

"Well, well, I dare say he's grown out of that. Mind the step, Florin, it's all broken away. Hold the lamp higher, can't you, man. Now, what did we come for? Port, yes, port. Now, there's some '96 somewhere, only a few bottles left. What does it say on this bin? I can't read. Bring the light over here."

"We drank up the last of the '96, sir, when the film-acting gentleman was here."

"Did we, Florin, did we? We shouldn't have done that, you know."

"Very particular about his wine, Mr. Isaacs was. My instructions was to give them whatever they wanted."

"Yes, but '96 port. . . . Well, well. Take up two bottles of the '04. Now, what else do we want? Claret —yes, *claret*. Claret, claret, claret, claret. Where do I keep the claret, Florin?"

Colonel Blount was just having tea—he had finished a brown boiled egg and was spreading a crumpet with honey—when Florin opened the library door and announced, "Captain and Mrs. Littlejohn, sir."

And Adam and Nina came in.

Colonel Blount put down his crumpet and rose to greet them.

"Well, Nina, it's a long time since you came to see your old father. So this is my son-in-law, eh? How do you do, my boy. Come and sit down, both of you. Florin will bring some more cups directly. . . . Well," he said, giving Adam a searching glance, "I can't say I should have recognized you. I used to know

290

your father very well indeed at one time. Used to be a neighbour of mine over at where-was-it. I expect you've forgotten those days. You used to come over here to ride with Nina. You can't have been more than ten or eleven. . . . Funny, something gave me an idea you had red hair . . ."

"I expect you'd heard him called 'Ginger,' " said Nina, "and that made you think of it."

"Something of the kind, I dare say . . . extraordinary thing to call him 'Ginger' when he's got ordinary fair hair . . . anyway, I'm very glad to see you, very glad. I'm afraid it'll be a very quiet weekend. We don't see many people here now. Florin says he's asked a Captain and Mrs. Something-or-other to come and stay, damn his impudence, but I said I wouldn't see them. Why should I entertain Florin's friends? Servants seem to think after they've been with you some time they can do anything they like. There was poor old Lady Graybridge, now—they only found out after her death that her man had been letting lodgings all the time in the North Wing. She never could understand why none of the fruit ever came into the dining-room—the butler and his boarders were eating it all in the servants' hall. And after she was ill, and couldn't leave her room, he laid out

291

a golf links in the park . . . shocking state of affairs. I don't believe Florin would do a thing like that—still, you never know. It's the thin edge of the wedge asking people down for the week-end."

In the kitchen Florin said, "*That's* not the Mr. Littlejohn I used to know."

Mrs. Florin said, "It's the young gentleman that came here to luncheon last month."

Ada said, "He's very nice looking."

Florin and Mrs. Florin said, "You be quiet, Ada. Have you taken the hot water up to their bedroom yet? Have you taken up their suitcases? Have you unpacked them? Did you brush the Colonel's evening suit? Do you expect Mr. Florin and Mrs. Florin to do *all* the work of the house? And look at your apron again, you wretched girl, if it isn't the second you've dirtied today."

Florin added, "Anyway, Miss Nina noticed the banner."

In the library Colonel Blount said, "I've got a treat for you tonight, anyway. The last two reels of my cinema film have just come back from being developed. I thought we'd run through it tonight. We shall have to go across to the Rectory, because the rector's got electric light, the lucky fellow. I told him to expect us. He didn't seem very pleased about it. Said he had to preach three sermons tomorrow, and be up at six for early service. That's not the Christmas spirit. Didn't want to bring the car round to fetch us either. It's only a matter of a quarter of a mile, no trouble to *him,* and how can we walk in the snow carrying all the apparatus? I said to him, 'If you practised a little more Christianity yourself we might be more willing to subscribe to your foreign missions and Boy Scouts and organ funds.' Had him there. Dammit, I put the man in his job myself—if I haven't a right to his car, who has?"

When they went up to change for dinner, Nina said to Adam, "I knew papa would never recognize you."

Adam said, "Look, someone's put mistletoe over our bed."

"I think you gave the Florins rather a surprise."

"My dear, what will the Rector say? He drove me to the station the first time I came. He thought I was mad."

". . . Poor Ginger. I wonder, are we treating him terribly badly? . . . It seemed a direct act of fate

293

that he should have been called up to join his regiment just at this moment."

"I left him a cheque to pay for you."

"Darling, you know it's a bad one."

"No cheque is bad until it's refused by the bank. Tomorrow's Christmas, then Boxing Day, then Sunday. He can't pay it in until Monday, and anything may have happened by then. The drunk Major may have turned up. If the worst comes to the worst I can always send you back to him."

"I expect it will end with that. . . . Darling, the honeymoon *was* hell . . . frightfully cold, and Ginger insisted on walking about on a terrace after dinner to see the moon on the Mediterranean—he played golf all day, and made friends with the other English people in the hotel. I can't tell you what it was like . . . too spirit-crushing, as poor Agatha used to say."

"Did I tell you I went to Agatha's funeral? There was practically no one there except the Chasms and some aunts. I went with Van, rather tight, and got stared at. I think they felt I was partly responsible for the accident. . . ."

"What about Miles?"

"He's had to leave the country, didn't you know?"

294

"Darling, I only came back from my honeymoon today. I haven't heard anything. . . . You know there seems to be none of us left now except you and me."

"And Ginger."

"Yes, and Ginger."

The cinematograph exhibition that evening was not really a success.

The Rector arrived while they were finishing dinner, and was shown into the dining-room shaking the snow from the shoulders of his overcoat.

"Come in, Rector, come in. We shan't be many minutes now. Take a glass of port and sit down. You've met my daughter, haven't you? And this is my new son-in-law."

"I think I've had the pleasure of meeting him before too."

"Nonsense, first time he's been here since he was so high—long before your time."

The Rector sipped his port and kept eyeing Adam over the top of his glass in a way which made Nina giggle. Then Adam giggled too, and the Rector's suspicions were confirmed. In this way relations were al-

295

ready on an uneasy basis before they reached the Rectory. The Colonel, however, was far too intent over the transport of his apparatus to notice anything.

"This is your first visit here?" said the Rector as he drove through the snow.

"I lived near here as a boy, you know," said Adam.

"Ah . . . but you were down here the other day, were you not? The Colonel often forgets things. . . ."

"No, no. I haven't been here for fifteen years."

"*I see,*" said the Rector with sinister emphasis, and murmured under his breath, "Remarkable . . . very sad and remarkable."

The Rector's wife was disposed to make rather a party of it, and had arranged some coffee and chocolate biscuits in the drawing-room, but the Colonel soon put an end to any frivolity of this kind by plunging them all in darkness.

He took out the bulbs of their electric lights and fitted in the plug of his lantern. A bright beam shot across the drawing-room like a searchlight, picking out the Rector, who was whispering in his wife's ear the news of his discovery.

". . . the same young man I told you of," he was saying. "Quite off his head, poor boy. He didn't even

296

remember coming here before. One expects that sort of thing in a man of the Colonel's age, but for a young man like that . . . a very bad look-out for the next generation. . . ."

The Colonel paused in his preparation.

"I say, Rector, I've just thought of something. I wish old Florin were here. He was in bed half the time they were taking the film. I know he'd love to see it. Could you be a good chap and run up in the car and fetch him?"

"No, really, Colonel, I hardly think that's necessary. I've just put the car away."

"I won't start before you come back, if that's what you're thinking of. It'll take me some time to get everything fixed up. We'll wait for you. I promise you that."

"My dear Colonel, it's snowing heavily—practically a blizzard. Surely it would be a mistaken kindness to drag an elderly man out of doors on a night like this in order to see a film which, I have no doubt, will soon be on view all over the country?"

"All right, Rector, just as you think best. I only thought after all it is Christmas . . . damn the thing; I got a nasty shock then."

Adam and Nina and the Rector and his wife sat in

297

the dark patiently. After a time the Colonel unrolled a silvered screen.

"Just help me take all these things off the chimney-piece someone," he said.

The Rector's wife scuttered to the preservation of her ornaments.

"Will it bear, do you think?" asked the Colonel, mounting precariously on the top of the piano, and exhibiting in his excitement an astonishing fund of latent vitality. "Now hand up the screen to me, will you? That's splendid. You don't mind a couple of screws in your wall, do you, Rector? Quite small ones."

Presently the screen was fixed and the lens directed so that it threw on to it a small square of light.

The audience sat down expectantly.

"Now," said the Colonel, and set the machine in motion.

There was a whirring sound, and suddenly there appeared on the screen the spectacle of four uniformed horsemen galloping backwards down the drive.

"Hullo," said the Colonel. "Something wrong there . . . that's funny. I must have forgotten to rewind it."

The horsemen disappeared, and there was a fresh whirring as the film was transferred to another spool.

298

"Now," said the Colonel, and sure enough there appeared in small and clear letters the notice, "THE WONDERFILM COMPANY OF GREAT BRITAIN PRESENTS." This legend, vibrating a good deal, but without other variation, filled the screen for some time ("Of course, I shall cut the caption's a bit before it's shown commercially," explained the Colonel) until its place was taken by "EFFIE LA TOUCHE IN." This announcement was displayed for practically no time at all; indeed, they had scarcely had time to read it before it was whisked away obliquely. ("Damn," said the Colonel. "Skidded.") There followed another long pause, and then:

"A BRAND FROM THE BURNING, A FILM BASED ON THE LIFE OF JOHN WESLEY."

("There," said the Colonel.)

"EIGHTEENTH CENTURY ENGLAND."

There came in breathless succession four bewigged men in fancy costume, sitting round a card table. There were glasses, heaps of money and candles on the table. They were clearly gambling feverishly and drinking a lot. ("There's a song there really," said the

299

Colonel, "only I'm afraid I haven't got a talkie apparatus yet.") Then a highwayman holding up the coach which Adam had seen; then some beggars starving outside Doubting Church; then some ladies in fancy costume dancing a minuet. Sometimes the heads of the dancers would disappear above the top of the pictures; sometimes they would sink waist deep as though in a quicksand; once Mr. Isaacs appeared at the side in shirt sleeves, waving them on. ("I'll have him out," said the Colonel.)

"Epworth Rectory, Lincolnshire (Eng.)"

("That's in case it's taken up in the States," said the Colonel. "I don't believe there is a Lincolnshire over there, but it's always courteous to put that in case.")

A corner of Doubting Hall appeared with clouds of smoke bellowing from the windows. A clergyman was seen handing out a succession of children with feverish rapidity of action. ("It's on fire, you see," said the Colonel. "We did that quite simply, by burning some stuff Isaacs had. It did make a smell.")

So the film went on eventfully for about half an hour. One of its peculiarities was that whenever the story reached a point of dramatic and significant ac-
300

tion, the film seemed to get faster and faster. Villagers trotted to church as though galvanized; lovers shot in and out of windows; horses flashed past like motor cars; riots happened so quickly that they were hardly noticed. On the other hand, any scene of repose or inaction, a conversation in a garden between two clergymen, Mrs. Wesley at her prayers, Lady Huntingdon asleep, etc., seemed prolonged almost unendurably. Even Colonel Blount suspected this imperfection.

"I think I might cut a bit there," he said, after Wesley had sat uninterruptedly composing a pamphlet for four and a half minutes.

When the reel came to an end everyone stirred luxuriously.

"Well, that was very nice," said the Rector's wife, "very nice and instructive."

"I really must congratulate you, Colonel. A production of absorbing interest. I had no idea Wesley's life was so full of adventure. I see I must read up my Lecky."

"Too divine, Papa."

"Thank you so much, sir, I enjoyed that immensely."

"But, bless you, that isn't the end," said the Colonel. "There are four more reels yet."

"Oh, that's good." "But how delightful." "Splendid." "Oh."

But the full story was never shown. Just at the beginning of the second part—when Wesley in America was being rescued from Red Indians by Lady Huntingdon disguised as a cowboy—there occurred one of the mishaps from which the largest super-cinemas are not absolutely immune. There was a sudden crackling sound, a long blue spark, and the light was extinguished."

"Oh, dear," said the Colonel, "I wonder what's happened now. We were just getting to such an exciting place." He bent all his energies on the apparatus, recklessly burning his fingers, while his audience sat in darkness. Presently the door opened and a housemaid appeared carrying a candle.

"If you please, mum," she said, "the light's gone out all over the house."

The Rector hurried across to the door and tried the switch in the passage. He clicked it up and down several times; he tapped it like a barometer and shook it slightly.

"It looks as though the wires were fused," he said.

"Really, Rector, how very inconvenient," said the Colonel crossly. "I can't possibly show the film with-

302

out electric current. Surely there must be something you can do?"

"I am afraid it will be a job for an electrician; it will be scarcely possible to get one before Monday," said the Rector with scarcely Christian calm. "In fact it is clear to me that my wife and myself and my whole household will have to spend the entire Christmas week-end in darkness."

"Well," said the Colonel. "I never expected this to happen. Of course, I know it's just as disappointing for you as it is for me. All the same . . ."

The housemaid brought in some candles and a bicycle lamp.

"There's only these in the house, sir," she said, "and the shops don't open till Monday."

"I don't think in the circumstances my hospitality can be of much more use to you, can it, Colonel? Perhaps you would like me to ring up and get a taxi out from Aylesbury."

"What's that? *Taxi?* Why, it's ridiculous to get a taxi out from Alyesbury to go a quarter of a mile!"

"I'm sure Mrs. Littlejohn wouldn't like to walk all the way on a night like this?"

"Perhaps a taxi would be a good idea, Papa."

"Of course, if you'd care to take shelter here . . .

it may clear up a little. But I think you'd find it very wretched sitting here in the dark?"

"No, no, of course, order a taxi," said the Colonel.

On the way back to the house he said, "I'd half made up my mind to lend him some of our lamps for the week-end. I certainly shan't now. Fancy hiring a taxi seven miles to drive us a few hundred yards. On Christmas eve, too. No wonder they find it hard to fill their churches when that's their idea of Christian fellowship. Just when I'd brought my film all that way to show them . . ."

Next morning Adam and Nina woke up under Ada's sprig of mistletoe to hear the bells ringing for Christmas, across the snow. "Come all to church, good people; good people, come to church." They had each hung up a stocking the evening before, and Adam had put a bottle of scent and a scent spray into Nina's, and she had put two ties and a new kind of safety razor into his. Ada brought them their tea and wished them a happy Christmas. Nina had remembered to get a present for each of the Florins, but had forgotten Ada, so she gave her the bottle of scent.

"Darling," said Adam, "it cost twenty-five shillings —on Archie Schwert's account at Asprey."

Later they put some crumbs of their bread and butter on the windowsill and a robin redbreast came to eat them. The whole day was like that.

Adam and Nina breakfasted alone in the dining-room. There was a row of silver plates kept hot by spirit lamps which held an omelette and devilled partridges and kejeri and kidneys and sole and some rolls; there was also a ham and a tongue and some brawn and a dish of pickled herrings. Nina ate an apple and Adam ate some toast.

Colonel Blount came down at eleven wearing a grey tail coat. He wished them a very good morning and they exchanged gifts. Adam gave him a box of cigars; Nina gave him a large illustrated book about modern cinema production; he gave Nina a seed-pearl brooch which had belonged to her mother, and he gave Adam a calendar with a coloured picture of a bulldog smoking a clay pipe and a thought from Longfellow for each day in the year.

At half-past eleven they all went to Matins.

"It will be a lesson to him in true Christian forgiveness," said the Colonel (but he ostentatiously read his Bible throughout the sermon). After church they called in at two or three cottages. Florin had been round the day before distributing parcels of grocery.

They were all pleased and interested to meet Miss Nina's husband. Many of them remembered him as a little boy, and remarked that he had grown out of all recognition. They reminded him with relish of many embarrassing episodes in Ginger's childhood, chiefly acts of destruction and cruelty to cats.

After luncheon they went down to see all the decorations in the servants' hall.

This was a yearly custom of some antiquity, and the Florins had prepared for it by hanging paper streamers from the gas brackets. Ada was having middle-day dinner with her parents who lived among the petrol pumps at Doubting village, so the Florins ate their turkey and plum pudding alone.

"I've seen as many as twenty-five sitting down to Christmas dinner at this table," said Florin. "Regular parties they used to have when the Colonel and Mr. Eric were boys. Theatricals and all the house turned topsy-turvy, and every gentleman with his own valet."

"Ah," said Mrs. Florin.

"Times is changed," said Florin, picking a tooth.

"Ah," said Mrs. Florin.

Then the family came in from the dining-room.

306

The Colonel knocked on the door and said, "May we come in, Mrs. Florin?"

"That you may, sir, and welcome," said Mrs. Florin.

Then Adam and Nina and the Colonel admired the decorations and handed over their presents wrapped in tissue paper. Then the Colonel said, "I think we should take a glass of wine together."

Florin opened a bottle of sherry which he had brought up that morning and poured out the glasses, handing one first to Nina, then to Mrs. Florin, then to the Colonel, then to Adam, and, finally, taking one for himself.

"My very best wishes to you, Mrs. Florin," said the Colonel, raising his glass, "and to you, Florin. The years go by, and we none of us get any younger, but I hope and trust that there are many Christmases in store for us yet. Mrs. Florin certainly doesn't look a day older than when she first came here. My best wishes to you both for another year of health and happiness."

Mrs. Florin said, "Best respects, sir, and thank you, sir, and the same to you."

Florin said, "And a great pleasure it is to see Miss Nina—Mrs. Littlejohn, I should say—with us once

307

more at her old home, and her husband too, and I'm sure Mrs. Florin and me wish them every happiness and prosperity in their married life together, and all I can say, if they can be as happy together as me and Mrs. Florin has been, well, that's the best I can wish them."

Then the family went away, and the house settled down to its afternoon nap.

After dinner that night Adam and the Colonel filled up their port glasses and turned their chairs towards the fire. Nina had gone into the drawing-room to smoke.

"You know," said the Colonel, poking back a log with his foot, "I'm very glad that Nina has married you, my boy. I've liked you from the moment I saw you. She's a headstrong girl—always was—but I knew that she'd make a sensible choice in the end. I foresee a very agreeable life ahead of you two young people."

"I hope so, sir."

"I'm sure of it, my boy. She's very nearly made several mistakes. There was an ass of a fellow here the other day wanting to marry her. A journalist. Awful silly fellow. He told me my old friend Canon Chatterbox was working on his paper. Well, I didn't like to contradict him—he ought to have known, after all—but I thought it was funny at the time, and then, d'you know, after he'd gone I was going through some old papers upstairs and I came on a cutting from the *Worcester Herald* describing his funeral. He died in 1912. Well, he must have been a muddle-headed sort of fellow to make a mistake like that, mustn't he? . . . Have some port?"

"Thank you."

"Then there was another chap. Came here selling vacuum cleaners, if you please, and asked me to give him a thousand pounds! Impudent young cub. I soon sent him about his business. . . . But you're different, Littlejohn. Just the sort of son-in-law I'd have chosen for myself. Your marriage has been a great happiness to me, my boy."

At this moment Nina came in to say that there were carol singers outside the drawing-room window.

"Bring 'em in," said the Colonel. "Bring 'em in. They come every year. And tell Florin to bring up the punch."

Florin brought up the punch in a huge silver punch bowl and Nina brought in the waits. They stood against the sideboard, caps in hand, blinking in the

309

gaslight, and very red about the nose and cheeks with the sudden warmth.

"Oh, tidings of comfort and joy," they sang,
 "comfort and joy,
  Oh, tidings of comfort and joy."

They sang *Good King Wenceslas*, and *The First Noel*, and *Adeste Fideles*, and *While Shepherds Watched Their Flocks*. Then Florin ladled out the punch, seeing that the younger ones did not get the glasses intended for their elders, but that each, according to his capacity, got a little more, but not much more, than was good for him.

The Colonel tasted the punch and pronounced it excellent. He then asked the carol singers their names and where they came from, and finally gave their leader five shillings and sent them off into the snow.

"It's been just like this every year, as long as I can remember," said the Colonel. "We always had a party at Christmas when we were boys . . . acted some very amusing charades too . . . always a glass of sherry after luncheon in the servants' hall and carol singers in the evening. . . . Tell me," he said, sud-
310

denly changing the subject, "did you *really* like what
you saw of my film yesterday?"

"It was the most divine film I ever saw, Papa."

"I enjoyed it enormously, sir, really I did."

"Did you? Did you? Well, I'm glad to hear that.
I don't believe the Rector did—not properly. Of
course, you only saw a bit of it, most disappointing. I
didn't like to say so at the time, but I thought it most
negligent of him to have his electric light in that sort
of condition so that it wouldn't last out for one evening. Most inconsiderate to anyone who wants to
show a film. But it's a glorious film, isn't it? You did
think so?"

"I never enjoyed a film so much, honestly."

"It makes a stepping stone in the development of
the British film industry," said the Colonel dreamily.
"It is the most important all-talkie super-religious
film to be produced solely in this country by British
artists and management and by British capital. It has
been directed throughout regardless of difficulty and
expense, and supervised by a staff of expert historians
and theologians. Nothing has been omitted that would
contribute to the meticulous accuracy of every detail.
The life of that great social and religious reformer
John Wesley is for the first time portrayed to a Brit-

311

ish public in all its humanity and tragedy. . . . I'm glad you realized all that, my boy, because, as a matter of fact, I had a proposal to make to you about it. I'm getting an old man and can't do everything, and I feel my services should be better spent in future as actor and producer, rather than on the commercial side. One needs someone young to manage that. Now what I thought was that perhaps you would care to come in with me as business partner. I bought the whole thing from Isaacs and, as you're one of the family, I shouldn't mind selling you a half share for, say, two thousand pounds. I know that that isn't much to you, and you'd be humanly certain to double your money in a few months. What do you say to it?"

"*Well* . . ." said Adam.

But he was never called upon to answer, for just at that moment the door of the dining-room opened and the Rector came in.

"Hullo, Rector, come in. This is very neighbourly of you to come and call at this time of night. A happy Christmas to you."

"Colonel Blount, I've got very terrible news. I had to come over and tell you . . ."

"I say, I am sorry. Nothing wrong at the Rectory I hope?"

"Worse, far worse. My wife and I were sitting over the fire after dinner, and as we couldn't read—not having any light—we put on the wireless. They were having a very pretty carol service. Suddenly they stopped in the middle and a special news bulletin was read. . . . Colonel, the most terrible and unexpected thing—*War has been declared.*"

HAPPY ENDING

N a splintered tree stump in the biggest battlefield in the history of the world, Adam
sat down and read a letter from Nina. It
had arrived early the day before, but in the intensive
fighting which followed he had not had a spare minute in which to open it.

> Doubting Hall,
>> Aylesbury.

"DEAREST ADAM,—*I wonder how you are. It is difficult to know what is happening quite because the papers say such odd things. Van has got a divine job
making up all the war news, and he invented a lovely
story about you the other day, how you'd saved hun-
dreds of people's lives, and there's what they call a
popular agitation saying why haven't you got the
V.C., so probably you will have by now. Isn't it
amusing?*

"*Ginger and I are very well. Ginger has a job in an*
314

office in Whitehall and wears a very grand sort of uni-
form, and, my dear, I'm going to have a baby, isn't it
too awful? But Ginger has quite made up his mind
it's his, and is as pleased as anything, so that's all
right. He's quite forgiven you about last Christmas,
and says anyway you're doing your bit now, and in
war time one lets bygones be bygones.

"Doubting is a hospital, did you know? Papa shows
his film to the wounded and they adore it. I saw Mr.
Benfleet, and he said how awful it was when one had
given all one's life in the cause of culture to see every-
thing one's stood for swept away, but that he's doing
very well with his 'Sword Unsheathed' series of war
poets.

"There's a new Government order that we have to
sleep in gas masks because of the bombs, but no one
does. They've put Archie in prison as an undesirable
alien, Ginger saw to that, he's terrific about spies. I'm
sick such a lot because of this baby, but everyone
says it's patriotic to have babies in war time. Why?

"Lots of love, my angel, take care of your dear self.

"N."

He put it back in its envelope and buttoned it into
his breast-pocket. Then he took out a pipe, filled it

315

and began to smoke. The scene all round him was one of unrelieved desolation; a great expanse of mud in which every visible object was burnt or broken. Sounds of firing thundered from beyond the horizon, and somewhere above the grey clouds there were aeroplanes. He had had no sleep for thirty-six hours. It was growing dark.

Presently he became aware of a figure approaching, painfully picking his way among the strands of barbed wire which strayed across the ground like drifting cobweb; a soldier clearly. As he came nearer Adam saw that he was levelling towards him a liquid-fire projector. Adam tightened his fingers about his Hux-dane-Halley bomb (for the dissemination of leprosy germs), and in this posture of mutual suspicion they met. Through the dusk Adam recognised the uniform of an English staff officer. He put the bomb back in his pocket and saluted.

The newcomer lowered his liquid-fire projector and raised his gas mask. "You're English, are you?" he said. "Can't see a thing. Broken my damned monocle."

"Why," said Adam. "You're the drunk Major."

"I'm not drunk, damn you, sir," said the drunk Major, "and, what's more, I'm a General. What the deuce are *you* doing here?"

316

"Well," said Adam. "I've lost my platoon."

"Lost your platoon. . . . I've lost my whole bloody division!"

"Is the battle over, sir?"

"I don't know, can't see a thing. It was going on all right last time I heard of it. My car's broken down somewhere over there. My driver went out to try and find someone to help and got lost, and I went out to look for him, and now I've lost the car too. Damn difficult country to find one's way about in. No landmarks. . . . Funny meeting you. I owe you some money."

"Thirty-five thousand pounds."

"Thirty-five thousand and five. Looked for you everywhere before this scrap started. I can give you the money now if you like."

"The pound's not worth much nowadays, is it?"

"About nothing. Still, I may as well give you a cheque. It'll buy you a couple of drinks and a newspaper. Talking of drinks, I've got a case of bubbly in the car if we could only find it. Salvaged it out of an R.A.F. mess that got bombed back at H.Q. Wish I could find that car."

Eventually they did find it. A Daimler limousine sunk to the axles in mud.

"Get in and sit down," said the General hospitably. "I'll turn the light on in a second."

Adam climbed in and found that it was not empty. In the corner, crumpled up in a French military great-coat, was a young woman fast asleep.

"*Hullo*, I'd forgotten all about you," said the General. "I picked up this little lady on the road. I can't introduce you, because I don't know her name. Wake up, mademoiselle."

The girl gave a little cry and opened two startled eyes.

"That's all right, little lady, nothing to be scared about—all friends here. *Parlez anglais?*"

"Sure," said the girl.

"Well, what about a spot?" said the General, peeling the tinfoil from the top of a bottle. "You'll find some glasses in the locker."

The woebegone fragment of womanhood in the corner looked a little less terrified when she saw the wine. She recognized it as the symbol of international goodwill.

"Now perhaps our fair visitor will tell us her name," said the General.

"I dunno," she said.

"Oh, come, little one, you mustn't be shy."

318

"I dunno. I been called a lot of things. I was called Chastity once. Then there was a lady at a party, and she sent me to Buenos Aires, and then when the war came she brought me back again, and I was with the soldiers training at Salisbury Plain. That was swell. They called me Bunny—I don't know why. Then they sent me over here and I was with the Canadians, what they called me wasn't nice, and then they left me behind when they retreated and I took up with some foreigners. They were nice too, though they *were* fighting against the English. Then *they* ran away, and the lorry I was in got stuck in the ditch, so I got in with some other foreigners who were on the same side as the English, and they were beasts, but I met an American doctor who had white hair, and he called me Emily because he said I reminded him of his daughter back home, so he took me to Paris and we had a lovely week till he took up with another girl in a night club, so he left me behind in Paris when he went back to the front, and I hadn't no money and they made a fuss about my passport, so they called me *numéro mille soixante dix-huit,* and they sent me and a lot of other girls off to the East to be with the soldiers there. At least they would have done only the ship got blown up, so I was rescued and the French

319

sent me up here in a train with some different girls who were very unrefined. Then I was in a tin hut with the girls, and then yesterday they had friends and I was alone, so I went for a walk, and when I came back the hut was gone and the girls were gone, and there didn't seem anyone anywhere until you came in your car, and now I don't rightly know where I am. *My, isn't war awful?*"

The General opened another bottle of champagne.

"Well, you're as right as rain now, little lady," he said, "so let's see you smile and look happy. You mustn't sit there scowling, you know—far too pretty a little mouth for that. Let me take off that heavy coat. Look, I'll wrap it round your knees. There, now, isn't that better? . . . Fine, strong little legs, eh? . . ."

Adam did not embarrass them. The wine and the deep cushions and the accumulated fatigue of two days' fighting drew him away from them and, oblivious to all the happy emotion pulsing near him, he sank into sleep.

The windows of the stranded motor car shone over the wasted expanse of the battlefield. Then the General pulled down the blinds, shutting out that sad scene.

"Cosier now, eh?" he said.

And Chastity in the prettiest way possible fingered the decorations on his uniform and asked him all about them.

And presently, like a circling typhoon, the sounds of battle began to return.